Too Many Jennys

Fifth Grade

JEN SHIMAN

Mermaid Café Books
9 Anja Drive
Simsbury, CT 06070

Book illustrations by Jen Shiman
Author photos by Liz Donnelly Photography
Cover Design by expertsubjects

Manufactured in the United States of America
Copyright ☺ 2020 by Jen Shiman

ISBN-978-1-7348842-0-3

DEDICATION

To my parents for the childhood gift of unconditional love, laughter, and the guiding principle to be myself. To my husband, Joe, and our angel babies, Madeleine, Ava, and Joey—for filling each day with the spirit of adventure. To Louisa May Alcott, Laura Ingalls Wilder and Maria von Trapp—women who remarkably captured the beauty and grace of everyday life—for inspiring my attempt.

By being yourself, you put something beautiful into the world that was not there before.

—Edwin Elliot

August 28, 1982

Dear Karen,

Hi! Your trip to Cape Cod sounded really fun. You're lucky it was so nice out. I feel like every time my family goes to Cape Cod—it rains! Cape Cod in the rain is completely terrible.

And I can't believe Jenny M. got a perm! I thought she was so against them. I haven't had a perm since your mom gave me one last October. I don't really have any curl left. My hair is a little longer than my shoulders right now. I want to keep on growing it.

So, school starts tomorrow and I'm NEVER going to be able to fall asleep (You know me!) Did you guys start yet? You must be so excited to be on the top floor! I always pictured us going up those stairs together. (Boo-hoo) Oh, I also DIDN'T GET MY UNIFORM! So, I have to go in normal clothes tomorrow. I am so mad. I wanted them to get here so bad and now I have to look like a complete weirdo!! The uniforms are red plaid. Our blue jumpers were way better.

It has been so boring here and I can't even wait one more second. This is torture.

Okay, well I am going to try and get some sleep (yeah right!) I wish you were coming with me. It would be so much better. I really hope I like it. Write soon.

Love,

Jenny

p.s.-I saw Rick Springfield on P.M. Magazine. Why did he do that to his hair?? And I hope there are cute boys in my class!!!!!!

CRETE

JUNE 3, 1982

"**K**ids! We're in Illinois!" my Dad announced proudly from the front seat. "We should be there in less than a half an hour."

I looked out my window hoping for something new to catch my eye but sadly, Illinois did not look much different than Indiana—everything was super flat and farmy-looking. We had been driving for eight hours since we woke up this morning. Yesterday we left our house in Connecticut, where the hills were all shapes and sizes and no two streets looked the same.

"I have to pee!" exclaimed my sister Lala. Lala was not quite five and was the absolute worst at limiting her drink intake. My mother had warned her at the last stop that she would need to "hold it" for two more hours. That didn't stop her from having three more ecto cooler-flavored *Hi-C* juice boxes.

"Lala, you're going to have to wait. There's no place for us to stop until we get there," stated my mother firmly, hoping Lala would not freak out with that news.

"Ohhhh. I'll try Mommy," Lala said, concerned. She sat on her hand thinking the extra pressure would help.

Lala was almost five years younger than me and I loved her. I sometimes called her "Fubsy" because that's exactly what she looked like to me—a "Fubsy" kind of person. She had the fattest cheeks that were often a bright red. Anything could really make them turn red—excitement, joy, cold air, hot air—but the best red was when she was in a stubborn mood. *Oh boy!* Her cheeks would turn a dark crimson as she would fold her arms in protest at whatever she didn't feel like doing, her eyebrows furrowed with fierce determination. We all found that very cute.

It was great having a younger sister even though we were so far apart in age, (I was ten) but she did cause me to worry sometimes. When she nonchalantly took out that last *Hi-C* a half-hour ago, I raised my eyebrows at her in warning. *You better be careful—that's a lot of liquid!* She had just looked back at me and shrugged her shoulders. *Who cares?* That was Lala. I was annoyed knowing that we would all have to live with the consequences of her reckless attitude—in this case, having to find a place for her to

8

pee when there was absolutely nothing but mottled grass as far as the eye could see.

Looking back out the window, I started to get a mix of excitement, nerves and anticipation at being almost there. It was becoming a familiar sensation to me—not having a clear picture of what was ahead. It was almost like when you were sick and you couldn't taste something that you normally liked. You knew it would taste normal again when you were better, but it still tasted gross now.

My Dad had shown us a few pictures of our new house. It was a brand-new, two-story home with light tan siding and a small, single tree out front. The tree barely surpassed the height of the first-floor window and it had two ropes propping it up on either side— Lala could probably kick it over. The house appeared to be the same size as our Connecticut house except they said it would have one extra bedroom. Lala and I had shared a room in Connecticut since my brother Kirk came along, so I was happy to have a room all to myself again. I looked over at Kirk who was still fast asleep in his car seat, despite Lala's uncomfortable "gotta hold in the pee" noises. *That kid could sleep through anything!*

Over the last two days in the car, I had way too much time to imagine what my school would be like and what cute boys there might be and now I was beyond impatient to just get there already.

This was going to be the third state that I would live in. I was born in Drexel Hill, a densely populated town a little outside of Philadelphia. Drexel Hill was where my parents were raised and where all my relatives lived. We usually ate dinner at my Ganny and D-Dad's or Mema and Baba's house at least three times a week. When my aunts would go shopping, I got to tag along—it was wonderful.

When I was five, my Dad's company transferred us to a town that was an hour and a half away. I was so sad to leave all my relatives, but after a while, I adjusted to my new home and came to love the country-like setting of Reading, PA, with its corn fields and rolling green hills. We did still get to visit with my relatives at the holidays so I could still see them, even if it wasn't as often as I would have liked.

Less than a year later, though, my Dad got promoted again, and we were off to Connecticut. Connecticut was almost five hours away from my relatives, which felt tragically far. After a while, though, just like last time, I was amazed at how quickly I could absorb into my new surroundings. While we didn't get to see our Drexel Hill family, I did spend more time with just my sister and parents and because of that, we felt like a solid team—just us against the world.

We lived in Connecticut from when I was in the middle of first grade until the end of fourth grade. My best friend there was Karen and we had so much fun together. Last year, we probably slept over each other's houses at least once every other week. We would make popcorn in her air popper—drizzling the melted butter on top and dance in her room to Rick Springfield wishing we were *"Jesse's Girl."* Karen loved Rick Springfield, had a huge poster of him in his black shirt and white suit, and thought she would just die if she didn't marry him some day. I was more interested in Tim LaBonne who was in our fourth grade class. He was tall, had sandy brown hair, a great smile, and was always cutely moving his eyebrows up and down as if to say, "Hi there, you like me?" I think he wiggled his eyebrows at just about every girl in our class. One time, he put his foot on top of my foot when we were sitting around the big table for our yellow level reading group. I thought it was just about the best day of my life.

My Mom thought I was way too young to think boys were cute, but I couldn't help myself. I just wanted to marry Tim. She didn't have to worry about Tim, though, because he usually spent his time pursuing Jenny M., who had the good luck of sitting by a window which would stream sunlight onto her gorgeous mane of long curly brown hair—making it look like she was an absolute angel. (It was no big surprise that she was selected by the teachers to play Mary in the Christmas pageant.) I used to fantasize about how he might love me more if I had the magical seat—lighting my hair up. Granted, my hair was not quite as long or curly as Jenny M.'s—but it still was a decent shade of brown that could look way better glowing from the sun.

In Connecticut, there had been three Jennys in our class—me, (Jenny F.) Jenny M. with the beautiful angel hair, and Jenny R. (Jenny R. was very quiet and you barely would even know she was in our class.) My mother had explained to me that there were so many Jennys, Jens and Jennifers because of the character *Jennifer Cavalleri* from the movie *Love Story*. The main character, named Jennifer, was naturally beautiful, intelligent and feisty which made the male lead, played by Ryan O'Neil, (who my Mom said was very cute but not as cute as Daddy) fall in love with her. No doubt, a good chunk of the 1972 moms were hoping their daughters would inherit these appealing traits if given the name Jennifer. I did really love my name, but I hated having to share it with so many other girls. There were always too many Jennys.

Suddenly aware of my surroundings, I realized that we were driving by more and more clusters of houses instead of just farms. Most of them seemed to be split-level houses with triangular looking roofs. Some garages even had decorations painted on them.

"Huh! Look at that, Tom. Do you see how there are designs on the garages? How odd!" declared my Mom just as I was thinking the same thing.

"Yeah, I wonder what that's about?" he mused. "Oh, okay, we are passing the last big road before we get there! We're so close!" He was truly excited about this next phase of our lives.

We passed a gas station on the left and started to slow down as my Dad made a turn into what looked like a colony of hundreds of houses.

"This is it, kids! Lincolnshire—After Abraham Lincoln."

"I thought the town was called Crete?" I said, confused.

"Yes, we are in Crete, but this is a development called Lincolnshire."

"What's a, Lel-lament?" Lala asked, repulsed. I agreed with her disgust—it sounded so sterile and unpleasant.

"DE-VEL-opment," Dad corrected. "It's just a planned neighborhood. Most were farms, originally, and the guys who planned it all out made the streets flow together, houses a similar style and some even have a park—this one does too, I think. We'll look later—oh, here it is, our street!"

Everyone but Kirk looked from side to side as we slowly drove up our street looking for our house. *This would be our street!* It was so strange that nothing was familiar.

"Here it is! 1089, Cardinal Lane!"

1089 Cardinal Lane looked just like the pictures I had examined at least a hundred times by now, but here it was—in real life. We pulled in the driveway and I noticed the little tiny tree out in front. Most of the houses on the street had similar baby trees propped up with ropes. You could kind of imagine how they would look when they were all grown up, but for now, they looked wobbly and unstable—like trees with training wheels.

Our house was really tight to the houses on either side—I could take five jumps and cover the space in between. I was anxious to see if the backyard was also tiny, but first, I needed to see the inside.

My Dad had our new key set in his glove compartment and he and my Mom, holding a still-sleeping Kirk, led us into our new house.

"Where's the bathroom?" Lala yelled.

"Right there, to the left," my Mom said as Lala darted towards relief. My parents had already been inside when they came to buy the house a few months ago before it was all finished.

I stepped into the hallway, which had a pretty staircase to the right, and looked up to the ceiling that travelled to the second floor. There was a little balcony-type area upstairs. *That would be fun to play on! Princess balcony? A store? Campout site?*

The house smelled of wood and paint—very new. Quite different from our last house in Connecticut, which initially smelled like boiled eggs. This was a huge improvement.

I walked to the right into a room which my Mom said would be the living room. *Boring!* Walking through it, we came to the dining room which had a little tiny chandelier. I spent about a second there and turned the corner and into a small kitchen with an eating area that had a nice big window overlooking the backyard. At closer inspection, the backyard seemed to be nothing more than grass with a very slight hill that ended in other backyards of houses. There was no barrier of any type in between. I couldn't tell where our yard ended and theirs started.

Past the kitchen and almost back to the front of the downstairs, was a family room. It had two double doors that led out to the backyard. It seemed very bright and cheery. *This will be my favorite room, I can tell.* There was also a tiny counter off the kitchen which opened into the family room. My Mom said we could get two stools so we could eat our breakfasts there. *How cool! I could eat my waffles there!* It wasn't a huge house—probably just slightly bigger than our last house, but it felt so new and modern that I couldn't help but feel proud and happy that it was ours.

The moving truck arrived just then, and the movers started bringing boxes into the house. Lala and I continued upstairs and I found my room which was on the right of the staircase, past the bathroom. My room had two beautiful windows overlooking the front yard. I did a cartwheel on the light-tan, plush carpet to celebrate.

Having my own room seemed unbelievable to me. I loved time by myself and tended to get lost in my imagination—so it was exciting that I didn't have to worry about Lala butting into my private time. I could pretend to be dancing with a prince or performing a legendary ballet concert and no one would know. *The luxury!* I also had two large closets. *Two!* My parents said they were going to use one—but I didn't care. *It looked cool.*

I could hear Lala screaming from her room and went to go see what the fuss was about.

"Jenny—it's *huge!*" she screamed, leaping all over the place like a jumping bean.

"It *is*, Lala. You have a great room," I agreed. Lala's room was a little bigger, but I liked the brightness of my room better. Also, it was right next to the bathroom, which was very handy. Now that my parents had their own bathroom, this one was pretty much for Lala and me to share since Kirk was still in diapers.

We kept exploring around as the movers rapidly deposited the familiar contents of our old house here in this new one. I found a little bathroom and closet off the hallway downstairs and a door that led to a double garage. Lala and I went to look around our backyard.

While the inside of the house was great, the yard was a huge disappointment. Our backyard in Connecticut was amazing—huge, surrounded by a wooden fence, lots of different trees of all different sizes and completely private. In the summertime, my Mom would fill up a pool and we would be happy as clams.

There was no privacy here! Everywhere you looked, there seemed to be a window of a house spying on us. They didn't even bother putting any training-wheel trees back here.

"Not the best, huh?" I said to Lala.

"Yeah! It's weird!" she agreed. "Let's do some somersaults on the hill." We went up the tiny, little slope of a hill, did two somersaults and landed at the bottom.

Unimpressed, we went back inside, and my Mom helped us set up our beds. Just as we finished, my Dad shouted from the hallway downstairs that he had a pizza. Our kitchen table was set up, so we sat around it and with Kirk in his highchair, had our first meal in our new house. We each had a *Sprite* with the square-shaped pieces of pizza and decided it was just "okay" and we should pick a different place next time.

"This feels weird," Lala said. "Weird" being her favorite word at the moment.

"It's pretty nutty, isn't it?" my Dad agreed.

"I know it's certainly going to take me a while to get used to little trees and designs on garage doors," my Mom agreed. "I don't understand that style."

"I don't like how our neighbors can all look at us. It's creepy!" I said.

"Well, you're kinda creepy too."

"Hey!" I laughed back at my Dad. "You know what I mean."

"I know, I know. It's going to take a while for things to feel normal again—but it will! I promise."

"I know. It just feels a little yucky now," I admitted.

"Well, tomorrow, let's get out and drive around, okay? That will help us feel a little better," my Mom said as we nodded. "For now, let's get you guys cleaned up and in bed. We have a lot more unpacking to do tomorrow and it's late."

"Okay," Lala and I said in unison, bounding upstairs to get in our PJs. Teeth brushed and face washed, I jumped into bed and surveyed my new room. I had decided to put the bed right in between both windows which divided the room straight in half—I was happy with that choice, felt princess-y. I asked God to help me feel normal as fast as possible, for there to be nice people here, better pizza, a fun school and a few cute boys would be good too. Maybe he could also arrange for me to be the only Jenny in the class. *Maybe?*

The next morning, I came downstairs into the kitchen and saw that my Dad had already gone out and got donuts for us. *What a guy!* I wolfed down a frosted all-chocolate donut first. Then, a Boston cream and a chocolate sprinkles followed. I washed it down with a big glass of milk. *Delicious!* My Mema was always saying I must have a hole in my stomach because I could put away so much food.

My sister and brother had a mix of sprinkles and frosting all over their faces and my Mom grabbed a towel to wipe them off before we left.

We all piled into the light green station wagon and got started on the tour of our new surroundings. We began in our development which was a big square maze —it reminded me of those little mini-pinball games. I felt totally lost as we were driving but knew it would make sense when I could ride my bike around and map it out.

We then set out for the Lincolnshire Country Club which my Dad said we were going to join. I had never belonged to a country club before— it sounded fancy and fun.

After five minutes of driving, there finally appeared to be an area that looked more like Connecticut with some actual normal-looking trees. "Look at those blueberries, Nif!" my Dad said, calling me his special nickname, as he pointed out some puffy bushes on the right. "We'll have to take a bike ride and come eat these!" That's one of the many things that I loved about my Dad—he made everything exciting.

"See how you can see so far here? Because there aren't a lot of hills in the Midwest, the sunsets are spectacular—crazy colors." As it was morning, I could only imagine.

We approached the country club, which was a big, beautiful, whitish-pink, mansion-looking thing. There was supposedly a pool out back, which we couldn't see—but I couldn't wait to swim in it! From there, we continued into the town of Steger, which was where my new school, St. Liborius, was.

Steger was much more packed-in than Crete—lots of buildings and few grassy areas. We passed a train track and my Dad pointed out Marvel Bakery on the left. "That's where I bought your donuts this morning!"

"Mmmm, they were sooooo good," said Lala with her eyes big from the memory.

It was a square, concrete building with a bright yellow rectangle covering the top of the building which read "MARVEL." A little sign was on the bottom window noted: Sicilian Pizza slices—$1.00.

"People come from far away, just to eat these donuts. It's a legendary bakery," Dad boasted. I found it strange that they made both donuts and pizza.

As we turned onto the street that my school was on, my Mom said, "Now Jennifer, I am worried about what you are going to think. It's kind of an old school. I hope you won't be upset."

The street was a boulevard and had trees—a few even a decent size—down the center. We inched up closer to a big, red brick, three-story building with a small cross modestly saluting out from the top. There was a big set of stairs right in the center leading up to the second floor. It resembled a big square head with windows for eyes and the stairs forming the long, bumpy nose. I looked at my Mom.

"Mom—I love it!" I gasped. I thought it looked beautiful and I couldn't describe the mix of excitement and anticipation at what my life would be like. *What will my teacher look like? Do we go into school in the front? Will I make an even better friend here? Will there be cute boys?* It was all so new and fresh—like my life was a book someone ripped in the middle. I just didn't know what those new chapters would hold yet.

The rectory was right next door and then, like a bookend, stood the church on the street corner—a gentle, rose-colored brick building. *It seemed safe.*

FIRST FEW WEEKS

June 27, 1982

Dear Karen,

Sorry it has taken me SO LONG to write! I am HERE! It's so strange to be here. I don't know why it feels so weird— maybe because I'm getting older. I don't know. Anyway—here is what I've been doing:

- ✽ *Went to the library and applied for my own library card. I already put some books on hold. There is one that had a cover with a girl with feathered hair. So pretty! Do you think you are going to get feathered hair? I want to.*

- ✽ *Put all my things away in my room. This took forever but it finally looks so nice! My Mom let me have their old velvet green couch—you know the one they had in their room? I put it against the wall, and I do gymnastics routines on it. I can lock my door and keep Lala out.*

- ✽ *Went to Klein's. It's a clothing store here that sells the uniform that I need for St. Liborius. Did I tell you it is called St. Liborius? Isn't that the weirdest church name you've ever heard of? The man said it may or may not be ready in time for the start of school. If I don't have it in time for school—I'll die!*

❀ *Rode my bike all around the neighborhood. It was so many streets, I thought it would take a while to figure out, but now I know my way around. My favorite spot so far is right up the street from our house. There is a big house down a long road by a pond. This is the only area with old, big trees that reminds me of Connecticut. There's a wooden fence against the road and I like hanging out there and looking at the water.*

❀ *Ate some really good pizza from the restaurant our next-door neighbors own, the Azzarello's. Aren't they lucky? Can you even imagine how amazing it would be to have your own restaurant? They can have pizza any time they want!*

❀ *Went to church at St. Liborius on Sunday. It is very pink marble-y looking inside. It's plainer than St. Bernard's. They have two really good singers—one man who sings like he's in the opera and a lady who sings so pretty.*

❀ *We joined a country club called Lincolnshire. It is a huge mansion looking building that is so fancy inside. You have to go through the building and super fancy dressing rooms to get to the pool. You are supposed to take a shower first. We did that the first time but gave up after that. The pool is kind of basic—just a big rectangle but there is a high dive and really good snack bar that makes amazing hamburgers and fat french fries. My Dad said it didn't cost too much to go there. I was worried because it seemed way too fancy.*

❀ *Met some neighbors. There were a bunch of ladies that my Mom was talking to a few days ago and they said I should try out for cheerleading and they were wondering if my blonde hair streak was natural. I guess they meant they thought I dyed my hair. I mean, I would get a perm, but what kid dyes their hair? Anyway, I may try cheerleading. It would be fun to get a cheerleading outfit.*

Well that's it for now. I hope you have a great time in Cape Cod!

Love,

Jenny

p.s. – Did you get any new records? I got Eye of the Tiger at the mall. I forgot to tell you that the mall here is HUGE! I wish we could go together.

Writing to Karen reminded me of how much I missed her. Up until now, I felt pretty excited with figuring out all the new places and restaurants and planning out how I wanted my room.

Now, I wished we were sitting on her big bed and deciding whether I should do cheerleading and how we would do our hair for school.

In Connecticut, I took ballet and played softball in my spare time. I really loved ballet and had been going to classes since I was five. Softball was also great—I loved hitting the ball and throwing it around in the yard with my Dad. He sometimes would throw balls to me that were a little bit out of my reach and told me to try my hardest to go for them. I was surprised when sometimes I could get some that I thought were too far away.

But cheerleading! It seemed so grown up and exciting. I loved costumes—getting my ballet recital costume was always the highlight of the dancing year for me. And a cheerleading outfit seemed equally as exciting. *Pom-poms—here I come!*

Mrs. Barlett told my Mom that practices started next Monday night at the elementary school and that there were no tryouts for junior cheerleading—I could just show up and do it. When we got home, I told her I really, really wanted to do it. So, she talked it over with my Dad and he said it would be okay.

Now all I had to do was wait until next Monday for cheerleading to start, get my uniform, and start school. Waiting was going to be hard.

3

CHEERLEADING

In the few days before Monday's cheerleading practice arrived, my Mom learned I could just go to practice in a t-shirt and shorts, but that they would be getting uniforms for the "Bulldog" cheerleaders before the first junior football game. The outfit was an orange, long-sleeved sweater over a white blouse and a blue and orange skirt. I was a little disappointed that there wasn't any kind of fun symbol or letters on the sweater, but the skirt and blue and orange pom-poms made up for it.

I put my hair in two braids and picked out a red shirt with the number three on it and a pair of white shorts. I thought that would look kind of sporty.

On the way to practice I asked, "Mom, has my school uniform come in yet?"

To which my Mom replied, "Jennifer! You just asked me that two hours ago!" *Oops. I guess I did.* When my Mom said "Jennifer" it meant she was annoyed—so I dropped it. But I really was getting nervous that it wouldn't get here in time! *What if I had to go on the first day without it? That would be horrible!* The uniforms for St. Liborius were a dark red plaid. My Mom had ordered me one plaid skirt, two white blouses with *Peter-Pan* collars, a red sweater, and three pairs of knee-high red socks. I was able to get the shoes right there and then—a pair of heavy, black leather loafers. Those were not very exciting. There was also the choice of the jumper—but that was kind of babyish—I wore that in my last school. Or, you could also buy plaid pants. I thought those looked majorly ugly. My mother was concerned about me keeping warm in the winter months with just a skirt, but I told her I would just wear tights and I would be fine. Anything not to have to wear those crazy-looking pants!

We arrived at Crete Elementary School, which was a really big, one-story building. We drove around the parking lot a bit until my Mom recognized our neighbor, Mrs. Bartlett. She was there with her daughter Meagan who had white-blonde hair that was perfectly curled and in two pigtails. She was a few years younger than me. For junior cheerleading, there wasn't really a strict age requirement. If you could remember the cheers and moves—you were in.

There looked to be about one or two other girls around my age and the rest were younger. One of the bigger girls came up to me and said, "Hi! I am Jennifer Barrow."

(Except the way she said "Jennifer" was more like JEN nee FURRR.) She had tan skin, a little darker than mine, and very thick, dark brown curly hair. It turned out she lived in the same development as me. She said her sister Emily was going to be one of the coaches. She went on to explain that they were from Texas and cheerleading was REALLY big there and that her sister knew A LOT about cheerleading. Her sister was going into high school, but she looked very old and sophisticated to me—like she could have been in college for all I knew. "I know what you're thinkin'! She could be my ma, right? She gets that ALL the time! People think she and my ma are twins." (She said "twins" it like TWEE-ans.)

I didn't really think her sister looked like she could be her mother, but I kept that to myself and just told Jennifer I thought she was pretty. Her sister's hair was dark brown and curled into the most beautiful feathered hairdo I had ever seen. "Feathered" hair was a hairdo that was cut on an angle by the face, so that when you curled it away from your face, it kind of resembled bird feathers. I had spent many hours at night dreaming about how my hair would look if I just could get it "feathered." Usually, I just wore my long, straight hair parted in the middle with two barrettes, pulling away the front part of my hair on each side of my face—like a curtain. I had a lot of hair and my Dad was always saying he wanted to see my face, so that was the hairdo my Mom had always given me. Sometimes in class, I would daydream about taking out my barrettes, shaking my head and letting my hair fall down around my shoulders. *Would the boys think I was more beautiful? Would they go crazy?* I never dared to actually take them out—that somehow seemed like breaking the rules—which I rarely did.

"Hey? Y'all ready to start?"

Big sister Emily was calling us over and we started learning a few cheers. She said we could start with three today and three on Wednesday, so that by our first game next Saturday, we would know six cheers that we could perform. "The most important part is to, one…smile, and two…start at the same time. Your leader will say 'Ready?' and you will say 'O-kay' and then you begin."

We practiced trying to get the timing of our "Readys" and "O-kays" down while smiling our biggest smiles. It was a lot harder than it looked.

The hour flew by and my mouth hurt from smiling so much. Before I knew it, my Mom was picking me up and asking how it was. "Pretty good. I met another Jennifer—she lives right in Lincolnshire! On Blue Bell Street."

"Oh-that's right behind us. You can probably see her house from our backyard," Mom said.

And sure enough, when we got home, we walked over and found Jennifer Barrow's house, which was diagonally right behind our house. My Mom was excited to have someone to carpool with and I was happy to have met someone around my age.

4

FIRST DAY

The day before school started was just like Christmas Eve to me. The level of excitement was just off the charts. Many kids dreaded going back to school but I always loved the first day. I mean, don't get me wrong—I LOVED summer. But there was just something about getting all your pencils sharpened and the stack of fresh, lined paper that just sent my brain into a happy place with the possibility of it all. *What will I write about? Will I have friends? What will they be like? Will my teacher be nice?*

I had arranged, taken out, and rearranged all my school supplies in my backpack at least ten times in the last few days. I practiced my cursive on a scrap piece of paper. My cousin Elisa had the most beautiful handwriting and I wanted to have nice handwriting too. Unfortunately, I often got impatient and then it would start to look pointy and all over the place. I vowed to try harder this year to have more even and round-curvy looking letters like Elisa did.

Earlier that night, my Mom made a great dinner of

chicken, white rice, gravy, and broccoli—one of my favorite meals. I took a shower afterwards and even blow-dried my hair so it would look smooth and shiny. The hardest part laid waiting ahead of me like a big pile of doom—trying to fall asleep.

I looked over at the yellow dress hanging on my closet. That was the only part I was NOT looking forward to.

"Jenny, I'm really sorry, hon, but they aren't going to get the uniform in until the third day of school," my Mom had unloaded the bad news in a regretful voice a few days ago.

"It's okay, Mom," I had told her. But I went up into my room, grabbed my favorite stuffed animal dog, named Popcorn, and cried into the pillow. I had been wishing and praying that it would come into Klein's in time. But it didn't and now I would stick out like a sore thumb. *New Girl alert!!* I was kind of used to the drill of being the new kid which was a combination and of awful and exciting—not knowing a soul, feeling alone, but ready for a new adventure. But I JUST wanted to at least look the same as everyone else. Now I would just feel like I had a gigantic spotlight on me, and I was dreading it. We decided the light-yellow dress was really pretty and it was kind of shaped like the uniform and even had a Peter-Pan collar. But when I looked at it again, I wondered if the yellow looked too different from red. *Would it be too sunny looking?*

I tried to put it out of my head and started to say

some prayers to God and Jesus. Usually, I prayed mostly to God, I don't know why. *God, please let this be a fun school. Let me have some nice friends here and help it not be so hard in the beginning when I don't know anyone. And if there are a couple of cute boys—that would be nice too. And help me to be myself. You too, Jesus.*

My mind kept wandering all over the place, thinking about my old schools, my best friend Karen and wondering what hairdo she would have for her first day. I thought about cheerleading and about how on earth I was going to eat breakfast the next day.

I got up and wrote a letter to Karen. We would have finally reached the second floor of the school this year—something we both were excited for. Grades 1-4 always lined up on the left of the staircase and went in first. Grades 5-8 lined up on the right side and they just seemed so much older and cooler. We couldn't believe that we were actually going to BE one of the older kids this year. But now we wouldn't do that together.

I hadn't written to Karen since my first letter when I got here and after finishing this second letter to her, I felt even farther away from her. She had sent me one letter after she got back from vacation, but I had no idea what she had been up to since then and I missed her. *God and Jesus, I hope Karen has a good year, but boy am I sad to not be with her. I hope I'm okay here.*

At some point, I must have fallen asleep because the next thing I knew, I opened my eyes and my alarm clock, which I had nicknamed "the bird" (because it made such a loud bird whistle for an alarm) was displaying 6:10 a.m. I had set the bird for 6:30 a.m., but I knew I would pop awake before it went off—on the first day, anyway. So, I turned the alarm off, brushed my teeth, went to the bathroom, put on my yellow dress and white, knee-high socks, brushed my hair, and put in the two barrettes on each side of my face.

My Mom was still in bed, so I went in and gave her a kiss and she grumbled, "I'll be up in just a sec, hon."

I went downstairs with my light blue backpack, poured myself some *Cheerios*, and added some milk and a teaspoon of sugar. Cereal was probably the worst choice I could have made—I should have gone with toast. Even with the milk, it tasted like cardboard—I was just too nervous and excited. I forced a few more bites in my mouth because I knew my Mom would make me eat more if she noticed an uneaten bowl.

She came down and made my lunch—a toasted peanut butter sandwich, an orange, a small baggie of pretzels, and a cookie. I usually always had the same thing for lunch—toasted peanut butter had been my favorite for two years now. It was cold by the time I ate it, but the toasted bread somehow gave it a really nice flavor with the peanut butter—even cold.

It was about forty minutes until my bus would come, so I went back upstairs and brushed my hair again. Then I tried to watch *New Zoo Review* on TV, but that show was really for little kids, so it was pretty boring and I felt like I would go crazy with anticipation.

Finally, ten minutes before the bus was to come, I went out in our driveway. I couldn't believe the bus would pick me up right here! My old bus used to pick me up a few blocks away—so this was a real luxury. (No more walking down a long road on rainy days avoiding the worms.) My Mom and Dad came out in the driveway with me and were all smiles—amused at my excited state.

"You're going to have a great time there, Niffer," my Dad beamed. (My parents sometimes called me Nif or Niffer instead of Jennifer. I liked it when I was little, but now it made me cringe a bit because it sounded so babyish. I liked "Jenny" better.) I just nodded back at him, impatient.

I kept looking in both directions. I didn't know which way the bus would come. Finally, I heard a rumble coming from the right—near where my new "secret spot" was. The yellow bus appeared and hummed like an imposing force down the road and slowed to an ominous stop. I gave my Mom and Dad a quick hug and climbed aboard.

There weren't too many kids on the bus yet, so I quickly found an empty row about three aisles away and sat down. I purposely sat on the opposite side as my driveway because then my parents wouldn't be able to see me. I didn't want them to see me as I went off—too on display.

The bus kept surging forward, picking up a few younger girls at the end of my street. It took a left and stopped for a boy who looked to be around my age—he had black, puffy-looking hair, a round head, round eyes, and round glasses. He walked by me and gave me a little half smile.

That gesture reassured me a bit. We chugged along, making one more stop on the main road to pick up a little girl with very long brown curly hair with a big bow in her hair. Everyone was wearing a uniform, of course.

We reached the now familiar boulevard in Steger where the school was and the bus slowed to a stop in front of the school. Here was where it always got tricky. I didn't know where to go and wished I had gone a few more rows back so I would have more people my age to follow. There were only two little kids in front of me and I didn't know if they would go to the same area I would need to go to.

I followed them out of the bus, by the side of the school—which was essentially a big parking lot—and to the back of the building. There seemed to be half of the kids lined up by the back door while the other half were running around chasing each other.

I noticed a bunch of people in lines looking at me—I even saw one older kid tap another boy, point to me, and say "Hey—it's a new girl, check it out." I pretended not to notice any of this attention directed my way.

I went to the adults at the top of the lines and asked an older-looking lady where to line up for the fifth grade. She directed me to the line next to her and said, "You can go right there, sweetie."

"Thanks," I managed to squeak out. I found my spot at the back of the fifth grade line, right behind a short girl with very long black hair worn in a ponytail. She had on the white blouse with the plaid pants. I wondered why she had picked the pants when they were so awful and said, "Hi, I'm Jenny. I'm new."

She said, "Hi. I'm Hope." *So there—the first person I met in my class. Hope. Almost like it was good luck— I had "Hope!"*

As I was feeling like, *"Okay, I'm going to make it!"* I heard, "Who the *heck* are YOU? Some sort of big *sun*flower? Hahahahaha." I looked over and saw an older looking girl slapping her hands and laughing. "Look at that, we got ourselves a little sunflower," she howled to some girls around her that didn't really give her a reaction but managed to look me up and down—half interested/half waiting to get in the door.

I just looked away and felt a huge wave of relief when I heard a bell ring. We waited a couple of minutes while the younger classes filed in the back door like a curved rope, and then it was our turn. I followed Hope in the doors, up a steep set of rubber padded stairs, into what seemed to be the large main hallway. Directly in front of me was another half set of stairs going back down (I imagined that must be to the front door.) and then there were four classrooms off the hall and another large staircase leading to a higher floor. We started moving to the room diagonally on the left. *Wait! If this school is first through eighth grade, why is fifth grade on the first floor?* Having the fifth grade classroom on the first floor was disappointing—I craved the grown-up feeling of the mysterious higher floors.

All of the kids in our line came into the room and a lady with light-brown curly hair, that was very short and tight to her head, said, "Just stand here for a moment, children. I will assign you to your desks."

She quickly called off our names as she stood by each desk. It seemed like she was going alphabetically, and I was relieved to be called in the second row, third desk down. I took shelter in my new space. The top of the desk was shaped like an apostrophe and underneath the seat was an open metal box where it looked like you could keep your books. I heard her say, "Jenny Travati" in the second to last row. *I'm not the only Jenny in this class—bummer.*

Once we were all seated, she told us that we could, starting with the first person in row one, come up one at a time, grab a carpet square and then go hang up our backpacks in the coat room. She instructed us to bring our supplies from our backpacks and just hold on to them for a moment. "These desks seats are really hard, so these carpet squares will make it feel a lot better for you," said my new teacher, smiling. *She must be pretty nice if she cares about it being comfortable.*

I went up at my turn and selected a tightly-woven

green carpet square with yellow stripes and placed it onto the seat. I followed the person in front of me, a short blonde girl with hair that was different lengths that was sticking out awkwardly in different directions, to the back of the room, past the teacher's desk and into a room that had hooks on the wall. There were no names assigned to the hooks, so I just put my backpack next to her spot. I mumbled a small, "Hi" to her as she was leaving.

She gave me a half smile and said "Hi" back.

I grabbed the contents of my backpack and went back to my desk, noticing how the carpet square really DID make it feel much more comfortable. I then felt safe to take a deep breath and observe some of the other few rows of kids moving back and forth from the front of the room to the coat room.

The class seemed to have an even number of boys and girls. A few of the boys looked cute. One had a nice face, curly light brown hair and crinkly brown eyes—like his eyes were smiling even though he wasn't. He looked shorter than me—but most boys were either my height or shorter. There was one girl with white blonde hair that was parted down the center. She had straight bangs, and then the hair at the top of her head was curled away from her face and the hair at the bottom of her hair was curled toward her face. It was a perfectly symmetrical hairdo, like a "half-feather." Her eyes were almost black and her expression looked naturally confident—she was both attractive and intimidating.

There was another girl that caught my eye. She was really pretty too and had long, honey brown hair—about five inches past her shoulders. Her bangs were curled down about half an inch away from her eyebrows and the rest of her thick hair was straight with the ends curled under. She had bright sparkly blue eyes, eyelashes that fanned out, and big dimples by her mouth.

I saw Jenny Travati go to the coatroom. She had blondish-brown hair that was a little frizzy and cut shorter in the front. Her eyes were blue and somewhat close together which gave her a sharp look.

"Hi class. I am Mrs. Transki, as most of you know," my new teacher said in greeting.

My attention snapped to Mrs. Transki at the front of the room. She looked to be about mom aged. She had a nice, reassuring smile and instantly made me feel calm. She wrote her name on the blackboard. "Before we get started today, I wanted to introduce a new student to our school, Jennifer Foster."

Instantly, thirty-something sets of eyes followed her arm which was outstretched in my direction. I tilted my head down to avoid eye-contact. *If they hadn't already spotted me and my "sunflower dress" they certainly saw me now!*

"I know you will all do a great job of making her feel very welcome here at St. Liborius." I heard a few people say "Hi" but I couldn't look up and just managed a meek wave.

She went on to describe what our typical day would look like, and all the normal first day of school type of stuff. Two things really caught my attention:

❀ Homework passes: If you completed all your homework for the week, you were awarded a homework pass. Although there were exceptions, you could use a pass to skip doing a homework assignment. *Wow! This was just so cool. I couldn't wait to get one and use it!*

❀ Jobs: On the back of the classroom door hung a big wheel with thirty triangles each with the name of a certain job. On the outer part of the wheel were all our names. Each week, Mrs. Transki explained, we would rotate the wheel a space. There were jobs like plant waterer, line leader, paper passer, recess equipment holder, window shade lifter, and bell ringer. I would later learn that, because fifth grade was located next to the buzzer that sounded the bell for the entire school, we had the unique privilege of being the school timekeeper. The bell ringer's job was extremely important, because they signaled lunch, recess, the start and the end of school. The fact that such a responsibility was bestowed upon us lessened the sting of not being on the highest floor.

The rest of the morning was spent organizing ourselves for the coming year. We covered our hardcover books with paper bags that Mrs. Transki had collected over the summer, wrote our names in folders, and collected notices to bring home to our parents.

Before I knew it, it was time for lunch. 11:30 was when the first floor went to lunch—which was perfect for me because I was always *starving* by then. Mrs. Transki rang the bell on this first day and showed the first name assigned to the position, David Rubinski, just how to do it.

We assembled in a line and headed back down the stairs with our lunches in hand. Once down the stairs, the line started to separate and it looked like all boys were going to the left, so I stayed with the girls on the right and followed the line into the girl's bathroom. *Strange!* Then, I noticed a few more stairs at the end of the room, and we seemed to be going that way. After those last five steps down, we arrived in a huge room that looked like a gymnasium. It had a stage on the left side, what looked to be a small kitchen off to the right, and a line of square windows at the top of the long side of the wall which was directly in front of me.

The room, which looked like it was used as a cafeteria, gym and auditorium, was half underground—so the windows were only on the top part that was above ground. All in all, it felt cozy and like this space had seen quite a history of school activities. *It had spirit.*

A tall girl with light brown hair from my class came up to me and said, "Hi. I'm Liz. Want to sit with us?"

I hadn't realized it, but I was just kind of standing off to the side—looking around at the room. I suddenly realized I must have looked quite odd! "Sure," I said, and followed her to a long table. I sat down next to her and saw that Hope, from earlier in the day, was there as well as the girl I met in the coat room.

Liz said, "This is Kristen and Hope."

"Hi," I said. I noticed that both Kristen and Hope, in addition to being very tiny, seemed shyer than me.

"Where did you move from?" asked Liz. Liz had short bangs, kind of big teeth, a small nose, freckles, and big, owl-like blue eyes. She had a real direct way of looking at you.

"I moved from Connecticut this summer," I replied.

"Wow! That's far away! What's it like in Connecticut?"

"Weeeell, I guess it's a little more spread-out. More farm-y. There are lots of hills, trees, and houses are a little more far away from each other. Like, when we first pulled up to our house here, it was weird that there was just a little baby tree in the front. I like climbing trees—so I guess it will take me a while before I can climb up that little guy." I had a quick chuckle thinking about it.

"I've lived here all of my life, but I have trees at my house. Where do you live?" asked Liz.

"um-Lincolnshire?" I had noticed how people from Lincolnshire said they lived "in Lincolnshire" rather than saying what street they lived on.

"Oh, Gregg lives there too."

"Who's Gregg?"

"He's in our class. Big curly black hair and glasses?" I just shook my head as I hadn't quite figured out who that was. Hope and Kristen didn't say anything. They were just quietly eating their lunches sometimes shyly glancing at me while Liz and I were getting to know each other. "Well, he's nice. The rich kids live there or further over across the highway."

I was a little shocked as I hadn't thought of where we lived as "rich" at all—nor had anyone I'd ever known called anyone "rich" before. Sure, it was a new house—and that felt super exciting—especially since out last house was pretty dingy when we first moved there—but it wasn't particularly very big, and I never thought of it as a "rich" house.

I was trying to figure out what she meant by it but decided not to say anything. I just mumbled out an "Oh," and then, because I was starting to get thirsty, I asked Liz where the milk was. She told me it was in the crate with a "5th grade" sign on it. My Mom had told me that she had already paid for half of the years' worth of milk and that I should go get some. I wandered up, feeling curious eyes looking at me, grabbed chocolate milk, and quickly went back to my spot.

When I sat down, I asked the three of them, "Do you like it here?"

Kristen and Hope replied, "Yeah" in unison. Then they kind of laughed that they both said the same thing at the same time in pretty much the same way. I could tell they were probably pretty nice once they loosened up a little bit.

Kristen went on to say, "I've had a lot of nice teachers here. Except for Mrs. Baxter. She was a little mean."

Hope chimed in, "Yeah-she IS a meany!"

And then we were interrupted by a whistle and lady telling us to clean up. I wouldn't get to hear any details for the time being about why Mrs. Baxter was so mean. It struck me that every time I moved, all the people I met had these shared histories. They all lived through Mrs. Baxter—the meany, but I would have to hear about it. That made me a little sad—I wished for that comradery that came with going through something together. Just when I would get to the point of feeling like I was part of a group, we would move. But, just as quick, I realized that there was not much I could do about it and, it *was* pretty neat to live in new places.

We went back up through the bathroom (*still such a strange way to get to a cafeteria/gym/auditorium!*) and outside to recess. Recess took place on the concrete black top which was used for parking when the school would have events. Everyone seemed to instantly spread out to the area they wanted to hang out in. There were some boys starting up a game of kickball. Some girls were off to the side of the building sitting down and talking, and a big group of older kids on the other side playing hockey.

I followed Liz, Kristen and Hope to a small grassy area next to where there was a kickball game in progress. I would have loved to play kickball, but I would have to wait until I knew more people. Instead, I listened to them talk about how different fifth grade felt from the babyish fourth grade with Mrs. Baxter yelling at them all the time. I didn't really have much to add here so I just tried to nod my head a lot and look sympathetic. Finally, we moved on to talking about our classroom this year. Everyone seemed to be excited about the job wheel.

"I can't wait to do the bell! But I don't know how I'm going to be able to pay attention to Mrs. Transki AND remember to keep looking at the clock!" I said.

"I know!" said Hope with much more gusto than I

had seen her from her yet. "I mean, what if we forget? The whole school will be off!"

"I guess those stinky eighth graders will just have to wait a little longer for lunch-haha," said Liz.

Just then the bell rang, and everyone started heading back to the door by the rear of the school. That got me wondering about who would ring the bell when we were out at recess? I guess Mrs. Transki would let us know.

The afternoon flew by with more subjects, rules and covering of books. Mrs. Transki gave us the breakdown of who was on each bus and we lined up, one bus at a time and headed out the door. I felt like my backpack weighted about fifty pounds as I headed out to the bus #38. There were three of us from my class on #38—myself, Gregg *(Aha! That's who Gregg is!)* and a boy that was in the first row, second seat in our class—Michael Bucknell. He had very blue eyes, super shiny straight brown hair and gave off a generally "nice" impression.

Sitting on the bus, I felt relieved that the first day was over but overwhelmed by the uncomfortable feeling that it was so much NEW to take in—me being NEW, learning NEW rules, NEW people, and NEW school work. It was so much to absorb and I was exhausted. I couldn't wait to get home and just plop on my couch and eat a snack. I was already starving again.

When the bus let me out in our driveway, I was overjoyed to be in a now familiar and safe place. Lala burst through our front door with her stuffed animal, Brownie, slung under her arm, and with one side of her hair in a pigtail, the other side having come loose. I can't remember ever being as happy to see her as I was at that moment and I pulled her up for a big hug.

"Mom made chocolate chip cookies!" she screamed with excitement—clearly bursting to share this news with me.

We ran inside together, each step making be feel happier and more relaxed and like everything was going to be okay. My Mom asked me to "tell her all about it" so I did my best to give her the details as I stuffed cookie after delicious cookie in my mouth. Just as I had gotten to "homework passes," we heard crying from upstairs and my Mom went upstairs to retrieve my little brother from his nap.

I didn't really have much homework except to have my Mom sign a few papers, so my sister and I played *Barbies* all afternoon on her bedroom floor and I enjoyed feeling like a kid and not having to worry about what anyone would think about me.

That night, we had cube steak, fried onions, peas and mashed potatoes for dinner. My Dad had given me a super big hug when he came home, and I felt like myself again—safe with all my family. The looming reality that I had to go back again tomorrow was a little tough to face down. I wished I could skip to the part when I had it all figured out.

THE GO GOS AND CUTE BOYS

I was amazed at how different I felt after just one week of school. Once the whirlwind of the first day was over, things just got easier and easier and I started to feel like I belonged.

My uniform had thankfully arrived by the third day of school and my Mom had it waiting for me when I got home. It fit perfectly and was a relief to visually blend in with everyone else.

When I would get on the bus each morning, Michael Bucknell would already be sitting about a third of the way down on the right. I would pick the row before him and he would say a very quiet and quick, "Hi, Jenny," as I would sit down.

I felt just as awkward and embarrassed as I imagined he felt and without looking, would squeak out a hasty "Hi" back to him.

Gregg, on the other hand, would bound into the bus a few stops later and plop down by us and say,

"Hi guys!" with lots of enthusiasm and as if to say *"Here we go again! At least we're together!"*

After that first day of school, no one would wait in line for the bell to ring—their backpacks would just mark their spot as kids ran around like hornets before they were forced to settle into the quiet of school.

I stuck by Liz, Hope and Kristen before school and at recess. Usually, we would just walk around and talk. They weren't a particularly active bunch but they were very nice. Hope was very small and looked like she could pass for second grade. Liz, on the other hand, was even taller than I was. She was all freckles and angles and didn't seem to be too coordinated— there seemed to be nothing that could prevent her from tripping. After just a few days, she had fallen UP the stairs, DOWN the stairs, tripped over a book by her desk, and even on Mrs. Transki's yard stick in the corner of the coat room. I wondered if she just didn't look down enough!

Kristen seemed like she hadn't run for anything her whole life. She was very happy to move slow and kind of looked like she could sink into a nap at any moment. I didn't feel like I had a lot in common with them, but they were the first people to be nice to me and I was so grateful to have some girls to talk to during these moments. Still, I would sometimes glance over at the games of catch or tag and wish I could be part of the excitement.

In the classroom, I was getting the hang of the routine and starting to take a few moments when I would finish work to look around and observe my fellow classmates. At my old school, I had a crush on one boy, Tim LaBonne. As I looked around at the boys in this class, there were several that I thought were "cute."

My "cute boy" list, which I wrote down safely hidden at home so I could send to Karen, was:

⚘ Michael Bucknell from bus #38. He is almost as tall as me and looks clean-cut and handsome. He always raises his hand in class and is always right. He doesn't seem to goof around as much as the other boys—but plays sports with them at recess.

⚘ "the twins"—David and Matt Rubinski. Both have very blond hair parted in the center but most everything else is different. Matt is tall, about my height, with blue eyes and looks big and strong. He is very relaxed and self-confident. Not like he is cocky or anything, just that he is comfortable and like nothing bothers him that much. He is usually at the center of organizing recess games, so I think most of the boys think of him as the leader. David is just as tall, but about thirty pounds less. His belt seems huge on him because his legs are so long and he is so skinny. He is always smiling, and a swirling ball of fun energy. I don't usually like blond hair on boys, but I like it on David.

❀ Mark Guadavere Another cute and energetic boy—the one I noticed on the first day. He has curly light brown hair, twinkly brown eyes, and looks like a human koala bear. You just wanted to give him a hug! Unfortunately, he is about two feet shorter than me.

❀ The only other boy is named Scott Clark. I was in line coming from recess one day and not realizing that I was humming part of *50 Ways to Leave Your Lover,* when Scott started humming along with me and said, "That's a cool song." He is tall with a more grown-up looking face and cute, but I am a little afraid of him. He mouthed-off to a teacher at recess one day, doesn't seem to pay attention in class and taps his pencils like drums at his desk all the time.

Other than observing the cute guys, I was enjoying my first job on the job wheel which was "milk crates." The task involved going into the kitchen, where there was a huge walk-in refrigerator, and grabbing the milk crate that was labeled for fifth grade. I would bring it to the first of two long tables where the fifth grade was assigned to sit for lunch. This also meant that I could leave our classroom a few minutes before the bell, so that the milk would be ready and waiting when everyone arrived.

I was also enjoying Mrs. Transki. She was kind and understood that we wanted to be treated like we were a little older.

She started reading us a book called *Flowers for Alegernon*. It was about a boy named Charlie with a very low IQ who was selected to undergo an experimental operation to increase his intelligence after the success of the same surgery on a lab mouse (whose name was Algernon.)

Mrs. Transki would read us about twenty pages after we got back in from recess. It really took the sting out of coming back inside to know that you could relax and listen to the story for a while. Even Scott Clark was completely quiet while she would read.

Another fun thing she would let us do, if we were well behaved for a week, was to pick out a song to listen to before lunch on Friday. The first song that the class voted for was *We Got the Beat,* by the Go Go's. I had never heard of the song or the band which made me wonder if they listened to different music here.

The song came on and it was all drums, rhythmic beats, and girl voices that sounded cool and confident. I instantly loved it. Everyone started moving in their seats—hands clapping, heads moving side to side and shoulders going up and down. I couldn't believe we were getting to dance (well, kind of) in our classroom. There was this palpable feeling that my life was going to be more grown-up here.

SLEEPOVER AT LIZ'S

A few weeks had passed and as I rode the bus to school, I was going over what had happened the day before:

"Wanna go inside?" sighed my neighbor, Jennifer Barrow, sounding very bored.

"Sure," I replied. I didn't want to go back inside. We had been jumping on her trampoline and doing the "jumping bean" which was when you both landed sitting down—one person landing slightly after the other—and the second person would then be catapulted by the energy and go flying into the air. I could do that ALL DAY. I never knew anyone with a trampoline before—and couldn't imagine my parents ever getting us something so extravagant. I guessed she had outgrown the fun of the jumping bean, so I tried to sound like I wasn't sad to go inside.

"Let's go in the playroom and play with my *Strawberry Shortcake* dolls," she demanded. Jennifer was one year younger than me, in fourth grade, and I think somewhere between fourth and fifth grade, you stopped liking *Strawberry Shortcake* dolls. With *Barbies*, you could still imagine them in grown-up situations like going to the mall or on dates, but *Strawberry Shortcake* was different. I didn't really know how to tell Jennifer this without hurting her feelings, so I just tried to play along.

After a while, Jennifer started throwing the dolls against the wall and making a big mess, so I said a little white lie which was that my Mom said I couldn't stay for very long.

"Noooooo-don't go home! You have to stay here and play with me. I won't let you go," she demanded.

I kept on telling her nicely that I had to go, and she kept hugging me saying "nooooooo!"

Eventually, I had to just pry myself from her and run out and say, "See you later!"

I shuttered thinking about how uncomfortable I felt. She was so pushy and I hated having to force my way out of the house. It made me wonder what I was going to do the next time I saw her. I didn't really want to be friends with her anymore, but I didn't know how I was going to avoid it when I saw her a couple times a week at cheerleading and she could just walk over my house anytime she wanted. I was at least relieved that she went to the public school and I didn't have to worry about being on the bus with her.

As we pulled up to the school, I saw Liz standing there and felt relieved to be spending the day with girls my own age. I couldn't imagine Liz throwing *Strawberry Shortcake* dolls at the wall like a crazy person.

"Hi Jenny! Guess what?" she asked.

"What?"

"My Mom said you could sleepover on Friday! Do you think you can?"

"I don't know…I hope I can! That would be so fun," I said, excited by the idea. The last time I had slept over anyone's house was at Karen's in Connecticut and that was probably four months ago. I always had so much fun at Karen's house and the idea of having that kind of close friendship again made me feel so happy.

The thing was, I wasn't quite sure I would like Liz as much as Karen. Karen and I just kind of got each other. I could just give her a look without saying anything, and she would instantly know what I was thinking and laugh. *Would I ever get there with Liz?* I told Liz that I would ask my parents and let her know the next day.

We were lined up waiting for the bell to ring as I saw Patty's bus arriving and kids filing out. Patty (the girl I noticed the first day who looked very confident) came out right before Matt and David. I wondered where they lived. Patty's hair looked perfect every day—super blonde and curled expertly. We were both in fifth grade, but somehow, she seemed WAY more sophisticated than me. I imagined she could have passed for a seventh grader.

I had been watching a bit closer the last week. (Never directly staring or anything—I didn't want anyone to think I was a weirdo!) Just kind of casually observing her when I could. She seemed like the boss of the girls and maybe even the class. Not that she blurted out orders or anything, it's just that everyone seemed to follow her lead. She was always sitting with Taryn, (the girl with the sparkly blue eyes) and some of the cute boys (Matt, David and Mike Bucknell,) often were hanging around her. Sometimes, I noticed she would make little comments under her breath and slightly smile with one side of her mouth. When she was talking to someone, she would look at them directly and would hold their gaze. The other person almost always looked away first—like an eye match of chicken. She always won.

"Do you ever talk to Patty?" I asked Liz in a whisper while waiting for the morning bell to ring.

"No! She's popular. She doesn't really talk to people like me."

I had heard the word popular before, of course,

but never in school. The way Liz said it, you would think Patty was a famous singer or actress. I was both intrigued and scared at the same time. *How did one become popular? Could I ever be popular? Should I stay away from popular people because they could make fun of me.? And if I wasn't popular, what was I?*

I knew enough that these questions would take a while to uncover. After all, it took almost half of a year before Karen and I had become friends, and these new mysteries would unfold no sooner.

"What about Taryn? Is she popular too?" I pressed further.

"Yeah. She's Patty's best friend. Patty's best friend used to be Emily, but she moved to Texas. So now she is best friends with Taryn. All the boys think Taryn is really pretty. She kind of does whatever Patty wants her to do. But she's not really smart, so sometimes Patty makes fun of her."

I couldn't imagine having a friend that made fun of me. I wondered if Taryn really liked Patty, or if she was just afraid of her.

The bell rang and we went up to class. I checked the job chart after putting my things away and saw that I was the "plant waterer" this week. *Fun!* I remembered that Mrs. Transki wanted the plants to be watered first thing each morning and before we left for the day, so I went into the coat room to grab the watering can. Michael Bucknell was in the coat room putting his raincoat away. It wasn't raining, but he seemed like the kind of guy to have it "just in case." He looked up at me and his cheeks turned red. He said, "Hi, Jenny," in a way that made it sound like he just admitted to a crime or something. *It sounded painful.*

I just smiled and felt a little bad for him and said, "Hi" back. And, "Gotta go water these thirsty guys!" *Oh my gosh! Why did I just say that?* I sounded like the goofiest person on the planet! I bet Patty would have just done a little cool smirk and said, "Hey," instead of blathering on like I did.

But then I thought, *who cares? I AM goofy—I can't pull off being as cool as Patty, so I might as well get it over with and let people know what I'm like—awkward moments and all.* I got some water from the fountain and watered the happy plants that decorated the sills of the six windows we had in our classroom.

When I got home from school that day, I ran up the stairs and into my Mom's bedroom where she was dusting the furniture. (My Mom always seemed to be doing something productive.)

"Can I sleep over Liz Crispin's house on Friday?" I pleaded with my eyebrows lifted hoping for a yes response.

"Liz Chicken?"

"Crispin, Mom. Not Chicken. A girl from my class. I sit with her at lunch. You know, she's the one I've been kind of hanging out with?"

"Well, I guess that would be okay—just let me check with you father."

Success! I knew my Dad would be fine with it so I already started celebrating.

My father came home later and said, "Sure, Peanut." *I knew it!* Now I just had to make it through the rest of the school week—four more long days.

My mother called Mrs. Crispin on the phone the next night and worked out all the details. I would pack a very small extra bag on Friday with my PJs, toothbrush, Popcorn and my cheerleading clothes for the next day. I would bring that to school, and we would walk straight home after school to Liz's house. Then my Mom would come pick me up around 10:00 the next morning so that I could make it to cheerleading for the junior football game.

When the final school bell rang on Friday, Liz and I just looked at each other and did a silent clap. Normally, I would have to wait ten more minutes until my bus came, but since I was a "walker" today, we lined up right away and headed out of the school. It felt exhilarating to be able to just walk out of the door and head straight home. *Liz was lucky*.

There were about fifty kids or so coming out of the door in little groups. Liz usually tagged behind her older brother Mike and his friends, but today, just the two of us walked down the road towards her house.

"We live just about three more blocks from here," Liz said after we were walking for a few minutes. That seemed fine to me. I loved the whole adventure of it. I noticed that almost all the houses looked the same in this neighborhood, they were long, narrow, two-story houses with a triangle shaped roof on top. They looked like pointy hot-dogs to me. Each block had ten houses—five right next to each other facing out, small backyards, and then the other five backing up to them, facing the other way. Even though there wasn't a whole lot of open space, there were huge beautiful trees lining the sidewalks.

We rounded the corner of the third block and Liz's house was the second house in.

"Hi Mom! We're here," blasted Liz. We walked into a small front hallway, through a wood-paneled family room and straight back into the kitchen.

"Hi Jenny," said Mrs. Crispin. "Liz has been talking so much about you. It's nice to finally meet you!"

"Thanks," I said, a little shyly.

"Now you moved from Connecticut, is that

right?"

"Yup!"

"Well this must feel much different, I imagine."

"It looks a lot different," I said, starting to warm up. "There aren't as many trees here. But I like how you have so many in your neighborhood."

"Okay—we're going to grab some pop and chips and head up to my room, Okay?" Liz said this more as a statement than a question.

"Okay, girls have fun," smiled Mrs. Crispin. I thought she seemed very nice.

I gave a little wave to Mrs. Crispin as we headed upstairs to Liz's room.

The stairs were very narrow and steep alongside the wall of the family room. As we got upstairs, there was a little hallway with a bathroom right in front of us. Liz's room was on the left—it had a slanted ceiling and also felt hot-dog shaped. There was a beautiful bay window that looked out to the trees. That was my favorite part.

"I LOVE this window! I would sit here all the time if this was my room."

"Thanks," said Liz, "I just usually sit on my bed."

Liz's bed was on the non-slanted side of the room

and was very girly looking—all pink and lace. It was funny because I didn't think of Liz as super girly. She didn't seem overly concerned about what she looked like and she wore uniform pants instead of a skirt.

She had a record player in the corner, and a few posters hanging on the wall—Cyndi Lauper, the Go Go's and the Chicago Cubs.

"Let's have some pop!" she declared.

The word "pop" was still strange to me. My family had tried to order soda at a pizza place the first week after we moved and the waitress looked at us quizzically and said, "you mean, pop?" That's when we learned that in the Midwest, soda was called "pop." Since then, it continued to give me an uncomfortable twinge each time I heard it, reminding me that I was far away from what was familiar.

"Orange or Grape?" she offered.

"Um, I'll take Grape."

"Sure! We have lots—so you can have the orange too later if you want."

She ripped open the bag of chips after taking a healthy gulp of orange pop and I noticed that both the pop can, and the chip bag were all white with a green and black stripe. The pop just said, "soda" and the chips said "potato chips" on the bag—nothing else.

"What kind of chips are those? I've never had them before?' I asked.

"Oh, these? They're generic," said Liz matter-of-factly.

"What's generic?"

"It's just the kind you get when you're poor. They don't advertise it or anything like something like *Coke* or *Fritos*. So, it costs less money, ya know?"

"Oh, I get it," I said trying to sound upbeat. I was shocked that Liz had called herself poor and hoped I didn't embarrass her. I hadn't really thought of her as poor. "So, what do you want to do?" I said trying to change the subject.

"Wanna make a dance routine?" she asked.

"Yeah!"

We spent the next few hours making up a routine to *Our Lips Are Sealed* by the Go-Go's. We'd do a spin off the bed, march a few steps, clap a few times, sing a bit and then fall into fits of laughter when one of us would screw up.

"Hey! Shut up in there!" growled Liz's brother Mike as he banged on the door, "and dinner's ready."

We came down and sat with Mike (who looked exactly like the boy version of Liz) and Mrs. Crispin around the small, round kitchen table. Liz explained that her Dad had the late shift which meant he was usually gone until they saw him briefly before school. The idea of that made me so sad and I thought about how devastated I would be to not to see my Dad and hear his jokes at the end of every day.

We had macaroni and cheese and red *Kool-Aid* for dinner. Now, even at my best friend, Karen's house, I never ate much in the way of cooked meals. If my Mom didn't cook it, I just felt squirmy about eating it. I don't know why. So, I just tried to move the food around a lot and sometimes would take bites and hold my nose and swallow it down—but it was torture for me. I was grateful we had eaten so many potato chips—otherwise I would have been starving.

Mrs. Crispin didn't seem to notice my lack of eating, so I was grateful when we were excused from the table.

We each got a popsicle and headed back up to her room to hang out some more.

I liked that Liz was always pretty much in a good mood—it made it easy to be around her. She was excited to get in our PJs and talk. We both took turns going into the upstairs bathroom to put on our PJs. I probably would have just changed in the same room with Karen, but I was starting to feel weird about undressing in front of anyone these days—even my little sister.

I had rainbow PJs which were starting to be short on my arms and legs. Liz had bright purple PJs with bright pink stars. Liz's bed was a twin, so she said we could both sleep on the floor if we wanted—which is what we wound up doing. She grabbed all the blankets and we made a nice new double-sized spot on the floor on top of her grey fluffy carpet. It was perfect.

"So, who do you think is cute?" asked Liz. Liz hadn't really asked about boys before—I didn't even know if she liked any or not and now, I was curious!

"Umm-I don't really know yet. I guess Mark is kind of cute. But he is so short."

"I know! He is a shorty! But I know what you mean—he always is smiling. He's always been nice—he never gets in fights with anyone. Unlike Scott! He is sooooo cute, but he is always getting into trouble."

"I was thinking the same thing! I mean, he IS cute, but I don't really find him cute anymore because he is scary too."

"Yeah—I still think he's cute, even though he's scary. Actually, I kind of like that he doesn't care what anybody thinks. He doesn't follow Patty around like all the other guys. That's cool." *Now that she mentioned it, she had a point!* Scott didn't seem to pay one lick of attention to Patty. He didn't really talk to many people in the class at all. I got the feeling he just had other things to do and was just waiting for school to be over. For the rest of us, our world revolved around school.

"So, do you think he knows you like him?" I pried.

"Oh—no way! If he knew it, I would die! You can NEVER say anything!"

"I won't—I promise! It's just, you really think he has no idea?"

"Nah—I only kind of look at him when he's not paying attention. Which is, kind of ALL the time."

At this we both burst into laughter.

"So, do you think Mark knows you like him?" asked Liz.

"No. not at all. At least I hope not! I don't really want anyone to pay attention to me at all," I admitted.

"Why not? You're pretty." I was surprised that Liz said that. I didn't really think of myself as pretty. Just average. My Mom always said I had a face that was "more mature" and that boys would notice me more when I got older. That was always very depressing to me. *What was I supposed to do with my face until then?*

"Oh. I don't think so, but thanks. I don't know, I just hate being new. I just want to kind of blend in, you know?"

Liz considered this for a moment looking at me very straightforward and said, "Well, if you say so— but if I was pretty like you, I'd just enjoy it and have guys fall all over me."

"You ARE pretty, Liz!" I said.

"No, I'm not. I'm a big freckled grasshopper. That's what my brother calls me," she said as she laughed at herself. She didn't seem to be sad about thinking of herself as a freckled grasshopper—just kind of accepted it very matter-of-factly.

"You are pretty...and your brother is a big dummy."

At that we both laughed again. We talked some more about Cyndi Lauper until I started to get very sleepy—I could never stay up very late. I said goodnight to Liz, pulled Popcorn out of my bag to snuggle with and fell fast asleep as Liz was telling a story about how Cyndi Lauper loved to change her hair color and she thought that made her so cool.

In the morning, we came downstairs and Liz's Mom was fixing pancakes. I was good and hungry by now and the pancakes didn't have anything weird about them, so I devoured six of them in no time.

Liz asked if I wanted milk and I said sure. She said, "It's powdered milk though, just so you know."

"What's powdered milk?

"It's the same as regular—it's just in powder form so you have to put water in it to make it whole again.

It's less money."

Instantly I was flooded with the panicky feeling of being too wimpy to try the powdered milk but worried I would hurt her feelings if I didn't.

Knowing I was a coward, I lied and said that I just wanted water.

Liz wasn't buying it and said, "It's just the same as regular milk. You don't have to be afraid of it, Jenny."

I felt horrible. I had hurt her feelings. And I just kept on with the lie—not knowing what else to do now. "Oh—it's not that. I just feel more like water."

It was terrible, this big lie hung between us threatening to ruin all the fun we just had.

We didn't have time to sort it out as the doorbell rang and it was my Mom coming to retrieve me. I ran upstairs to grab my stuff quickly and change into my cheerleading clothes.

I blurted a clipped "thank you" to Liz and her Mom and was relieved to get away from the uncomfortable situation. I left feeling so ashamed for how I had reacted and worried that Liz would look at me differently the next time I saw her.

September 30, 1982

Dear Karen,

Hi! What's up? Sorry I didn't write back right away. I can't believe that Yvonne likes Tim now. I am a little mad, but I guess it's not fair of me to be mad because I don't even live there anymore, and she didn't even know that I liked him. Do you think he actually likes her? I feel like they would be so weird together. I also can't picture her with longer hair. It's been short forever.

How is tap going? I miss ballet. The closest place they have around here is almost an hour away. My mom doesn't want to do it because it's just too far to drive Lala and Kirk and she doesn't want to leave them alone. Cheerleading is almost done—it's been kind of boring. I don't really know most of the girls because they go to the public school and all the boys on the team go to there too. So, it's kind of stupid to be cheering for people you barely know. I don't think I'll do it again.

I had a sleepover with this girl, Liz. She is pretty nice, and I like her—but I can't picture myself EVER being best friends with her like I am with you. She is just too different from me. Like, she likes the same type of music and everything, but she isn't super girly and doesn't really like to do hair and play with makeup and stuff like that. She also doesn't really do any sports or anything and I am dying to play with the guys at recess. It is so boring just standing around talking.

Remember that day at recess when we kept trying to be blood sisters and pricking our finger with a safety pin, but we kept chickening out and then Sister Grace came over and asked us what we were doing, and we got so scared? Hahahahaha. That was so funny.

Well, not much else going on around here. Write me soon and let me know what's going on.

Love,

Jenny

p.s.-Lala told our neighbors that Kirk was in the hospital and they came over and brought a chicken noodle thingy and my Mom was so embarrassed and mad at Lala. She got in so much trouble. She is one crazy sister!

p.p.s- I put in my world-famous list of cute guys.

THE QUESTION

Back at school on Monday, Liz was the same as normal. *Relief!* I was worried she would still feel insulted that I didn't drink the powdered milk. We played Chinese jump rope while we were waiting to go into school and she told me how her brother was such a jerk complaining that she's never allowed to have sleepovers anymore because we were so loud. I didn't really think we were very loud, and I was glad I didn't have an older brother to give me a hard time.

This week I had the job of "paper passer." Anytime Mrs. Transki needed anything passed out, I was the girl. In addition to passing out blank papers to the top of each row, the job also included returning graded homework. After you were the "paper passer," you had a pretty good idea of who was smart (Michael Bucknell, Matt and David Rubinski and a tall, quiet girl named, Kathy Spritzer,) and who struggled (Taryn Wentworth, Scott Clark and Trevor Miller.) Everyone else in class seemed to be somewhere in the middle. I usually did well in school, but lately I would find myself observing other people so much that I would forget to pay attention to my teacher. As a result, my homework and quizzes would usually have one or two things wrong.

Homework passes were the most fun thing to pass out. They were given out on Mondays for having successfully turned in all work from the previous week. Mrs. Transki created homework passes by taking a colored piece of construction paper, cutting it into four equal pieces, stamping it with a picture—this week a frog jumping off a lily pad under the words "Great Job!—and then signing her name and dating it. When you were the paper passer and dropped off the homework passes, you'd always get a little cheer. It was fun to be the deliverer of good news.

Last week a girl named Shelly was the paper passer. I hadn't really noticed Shelly that much yet—she really kept to herself and would sit at lunch with Kathy. Shelly had very curly black hair that went down a few inches past her shoulders. She had big curly bangs and would usually put a few barrettes in the front of her hair to keep it out of her face. But instead of pulling her hair to the side of her face, like I did, Shelly would take her hair straight back—kind of like two straight lines coming out of her bangs. She had a very pale skin and her cheeks always were a crimson shade of pink. She also was the only girl in our class who had, as my Mom would say, "developed." I guessed that she felt very embarrassed to be so developed as she was always hunching her shoulders to avoid attention of her grown-up looking body. If Patty could pass for seventh grade, I bet

Shelly could even be mistaken for an eighth grader!

Another thing I noticed about Shelly was that she was the most graceful person I had ever seen. Something about the way she passed out paper completely mesmerized me. She moved so quietly, and when she got to someone's desk, she would gently take the paper from the pile and, with the most elegant flip of the wrist, gently float it on the corner of the desk. I don't know why it looked so appealing—but it did.

That Tuesday, as I was passing back Patty's homework, she held me at her desk by putting her hand firmly on top my hand and whispered, "Jenny— Mike Bucknell wants you to go to the Starflyer with him this weekend. We're all going. You should go with." Then she released her grip over my hand.

I just kind of nodded my head and kept passing out homework—but I was in shock.

First of all, that was about the first time that Patty had ever said anything to me. Second, what was the Starflyer? Sledding? But, there wasn't any snow yet. And third, Michael Bucknell wanted to go somewhere with me? I couldn't believe it. I felt my face get very hot and was relieved when I could sit back down.

Mrs. Transki got up from her desk in the back corner of the room and went to the front of the classroom to start our social studies lesson on

Canada.

Patty made a "psst" sound in my direction, so I looked over. She mouthed, "I'll tell you about it at recess."

I did a quick nod and got back to the business of pretending I was interested in the natural resources of Canada.

Michael Bucknell wanted to go somewhere with me? I couldn't believe it. I thought he was really nice, but I hadn't really been thinking about him as much as Mark. But then I just started to feel so tingly and excited. I couldn't believe that a boy liked me! I mean, I suppose he probably liked me if he wanted to go somewhere with me. *Was the Starflyer the movies?* Oh, I hoped it wasn't the moves—I didn't think my parents would let me go.

"Jenny?" asked Mrs. Transki.

"Huh?" I suddenly mumbled, realizing the class was looking at me.

"I was just asking if you had a question."

"Me? Oh, no...no question...just learning about Canada." *Oh my gosh—did I actually just say that out loud?*

"It looked like your hand was up, that's all," said Mrs. Transki, eying me strangely—trying to figure out why I was acting so odd.

I realized that I was leaning on my arm with my hand by my head and promptly tucked it down by my lap.

"Nope. Just resting my head." *Why? Why did I have to keep saying weird things out loud?* I wanted to slink into a hole.

The remaining time between social studies and lunch crawled by excruciatingly slow. I tried my very hardest to focus on what Mrs. Transki was saying because I did not want to be called out again in front of the class. *This was torture! How was I supposed to stop thinking about what the Starflyer was, if I could go, and that Mike Bucknell wanted to go with me?*

Mercifully, lunch eventually came, and I wolfed down my tasteless peanut butter sandwich. Normally, I would have savored every bite, but I was WAY too excited to have my taste buds work.

I didn't tell Liz and the girls about what Patty had said. I was worried that maybe I was being tricked somehow and I would just wind up looking dumb. I also didn't know how they would react to me telling them that Patty had talked to me. *Would they be mad at me?* Patty never talked to them.

When we went outside for recess, I didn't really know what to do. *Should I go up to Patty? Should I wait for her to come to me?* I decided I should wait for her to come to me, that was safer.

After a couple of minutes, Patty and Taryn wandered over and Patty said, "Jenny, come here."

I just looked at Liz, Hope and Kristen and lifted my eyebrows to somehow signal to them that I didn't know what to do, but should probably go. They just looked back at me like they were puzzled, but knew I had to go. It's not like Patty had asked if I *wanted* to come over. It was a command, *come here*, and the rest of us were too weak to question someone as confident as Patty.

Patty, Taryn and I walked over to by the side of the school by the fire escape. As soon as we were safely by ourselves, Patty turned to me with her level gaze and said, "You are going to die. Mike Bucknell wants you to go with him when we go to the Starflyer this Saturday. You HAVE to go. He is the best. You know he likes you, right?" she said as a challenge.

My head started to swirl, and I couldn't really process all this information at once. All I could manage to get out was, "Um, not really. What is the Starflyer?"

I knew this probably sounded so dumb to Patty and that, if I was any kind of cool girl, I would know what the Starflyer was. But I really needed to know because I couldn't ask my parents to go if I didn't know what it was.

Patty honked out a laugh and looked at me like I was just a baby. "It's the *roller-skating* rink, Jenny! We go almost *every* Saturday. It's from one to four. My Mom drives us. You *have* to go with, or Mike will die."

"Um, well, I'll try. I have to ask my parents," I confessed knowing that the fact that I had to ask my parents was probably very babyish—I imagine Patty probably just declared she was going to her parents.

Surprisingly, Patty looked sympathetic and said, "Just have your Mom call my Mom. It will work. So, you knew he liked you though, right?"

"No, not really—he's just on my bus and is nice," I admitted, as my eyes searched the ground and my face got hot.

Patty laughed again, "Well, we go as a group, but Mike will want to skate with you at couples' skate. I skate with Matt and Taryn skates with David."

Taryn, who hadn't said a word the whole time, just looked at me and smiled, causing her dimples to pop. *She was SO pretty—even more so from this close.* She had bright blue eyes that seemed to sparkle with long black lashes that stuck straight out like a fan. Something about her smile reassured me that she was on my side. Or, at least, she wasn't out to get me or make fun of me.

Patty continued, "So have your Mom call my Mom tonight, okay?"

"Okay," I agreed, and feeling like I was dismissed, turned around and went back to the safety of Liz,

Hope and Kristen.

"What did she want?" asked Liz. I nonchalantly looked around, pretending to be looking for something and saw that Patty and Taryn had walked back to where the boys were playing kickball. They were not looking in my direction.

"Um. Well—I guess they are going to the Starflyer and Michael wants me to go?" I said this like I couldn't believe it, which I really still couldn't.

Liz, Hope and Kristen's eyes all got huge at the same time. "Whoa! Michael Bucknell! Do you like him?" blurted Liz, "I thought you liked Mark?"

"Um. I don't know. I haven't really thought about it. I mean, I guess Michael's nice and all," I admitted.

"So, are you going to go?" asked Liz sounding part disbelieving of my luck and part proud.

"I've never really gone anywhere with a boy before. I don't know if my parents will let me." I was honest. I actually was becoming very upset at the thought that I really was starting to want to go but wouldn't be allowed to go.

The bell rang and we hustled back into class. A mix of emotions swirled through my head— excitement at the thought of going and having a boy like me, dread at the thought of asking my parents, and worry that I would hurt Liz, Hope and Kristen's feeling by being invited to something that hadn't been asked to do.

When bus #38 was called at the end of the day, I made sure I got into line first. I didn't want to make eye contact with Michael—the thought of it just about made me want to die of embarrassment.

Once I was safely wedged against the window in my seat, I saw him go by me out of the corner of my eye. He must have known that Patty had asked me by now. *Was he as nervous as I was?*

I practically leaped out of the bus when we got to my house, and I ran up our small front yard and in the door—thinking every second I got in the door faster, was a second that Mike Bucknell could not look at me out of the bus window.

My brother was always sleeping at this time of day, so I tried to be quiet as I went through the family room looking for my Mom.

I found her in the kitchen, sitting at our table and looking up a recipe in the big, worn, Julia Child cookbook. "Hi hon! How was school?"

I wished that somehow, I could just communicate telepathically with her, so I didn't actually have to say out loud that I wanted to go to the Starflyer with a group of kids—some of them being boys. I was terrified that she would see that I was excited to go, and she would be disappointed in me for liking boys.

I wanted to be uninterested in boys like she was at my age, but I honestly couldn't even remember a time when I didn't have a list of cute boys in my head. *What was wrong with me? Was I normal?*

I took a deep breath knowing that if I wanted to go, I would just have to fess up. "Well, it was kind of a crazy day, Mom."

"Really? Why?" She turned away from the book to look at me.

"Well, one of the girls in my class, Patty, asked if I wanted to go to this roller-skating place on Saturday with a group of kids from the class." *There! I got it out! And it didn't sound so bad to my ears.*

But she knew! "Just girls?" she pressed.

"Um…well, I think there are *some* boys going?" I said this like I didn't know for sure. "But it's just a group."

"Oh…hmm….I don't know if you are old enough to be going to boy-girl things," she mused with her eyebrows furrowed, thinking it over.

"Patty said you could call her Mom and talk to her. I don't really know Patty that well."

"You don't? How come you want to go then?"

"Um, I dunno, I guess it would be fun," I said, trying not to sound too anxious.

"Well, I don't know, Jennifer. I'll have to talk to your father about it," she decided.

Normally, this would have been great news. My Dad was usually fine with me doing anything that was for fun. My Mom always weighed out the cost and whether she could work it in with my brother's naps and such. But this was different. *Boys* would be there. *Would my Dad be horrified? Would he think I am horrible for wanting to go somewhere with boys?* The thought of not knowing what his reaction would be almost made me want to take it back. But I did *really* want to go. I would just have to wait until he got home to find out.

After two and a half hours of staring at my homework, doing somersaults on my green couch, and trying out hairdos in front of my mirror, I heard his car pull in and him lifting the garage door. I leaped into bed, pulled a blanket over my head and pretended to be asleep. Somehow, I thought, if they came to tell me their decision, and I was sleeping in bed, it must mean that I am not very excited about going and therefore must not like boys.

After ten minutes, my Mom knocked on my door as I pretended to be woken up saying, "come in" in my sleepiest voice.

Both my Mom and Dad came in and sat on my bed. My Mom said, "Jenny, Daddy and I talked, and we are going to let you go skating with the group. But we want you to promise to be on your best behavior, Okay? This is the first time you will be going with boys and no parents will be there."

"Oh—I mean, I'm not going to hang out with boys or anything. They are just going to be there," I said desperately trying still to come off as uninterested.

"Have fun, Peanut. Just be careful, okay?" said my Dad. He looked slightly tortured—or maybe I was just so worried that he was disappointed in me I imagined it to be true.

Still pretending not to be too excited, I said, "Okay, thanks. I promise everything will be fine. I just want to go skate—it sounds kind of fun."

They gave me a little hug and I was so relieved to have this discussion over with. My Mom said dinner was ready—meatloaf and baked potatoes. Suddenly, I was ravenous and ran downstairs to eat a huge, satisfying dinner.

STARFLYER

My Mom had called Patty's mom that night and had a nice talk. She felt a lot better about me going skating after Patty's mom assured her it was a nice group of boys and girls and she knew all the parents very well. Especially the Rubinski's—they were just down the road and she had known the twins and their parents since they were babies.

I felt the need to report back to Patty that I could go the next day, even though I knew she would have found out already from her mom. "Good," she declared. "Mike will be happy. He is such a great kid." I thought it strange that she called him a kid when we were all the same age, but somehow, she could pull that off. She also was the only one who called him Mike—everyone else called him Michael. "So, what are you going to wear?" she asked.

Oh boy. I hadn't even thought about that! "Uh. I dunno, I haven't really thought about it," I confessed.

"Well, I'll probably wear my *Gloria Vanderbilt* jeans

and a sweater." I didn't know what *Gloria Vanderbilt* jeans were, so I just nodded like I did.

"I get kind of hot, so I might just wear a t-shirt," Taryn added innocently.

"Just make sure it doesn't have unicorns on it!" honked Patty laughing about something that must have happened before with some poor soul (*Taryn?*) wearing a unicorn shirt that Patty deemed dorky.

Taryn just smiled. Then Patty looked back at me. "So, have you told Mike you are going?"

Oh no! Was I going to have to tell Michael I was going? I was hoping he would just find out from Patty! "No, um, not really, no," I mumbled nervously.

Patty laughed her cool laugh—already seeming to know I would say that. "Don't worry. I told Matt you were coming—so I'm sure he already told Mike. But you should tell him too."

Oh dread. Why? Why did I have to tell him? Was Patty just trying to torture me? This was going to be horrible.

Later that day before we were going to lunch Patty summoned me over when she, Matt and David were getting their coats on. She also called over to Michael.

"Jenny—did you want to tell Mike?" *Oh my goodness. Could this really be happening?* Instantly, I felt sweaty. I peeked over at Michael, who I had not made eye contact with for a couple of days now and saw that his face was red too.

"Oh…um…yeah, so…I'm going to go with you guys," I mustered with as much nonchalance as I could pull off.

"Oh, nice," he replied. "I'll see you guys later; I have to go get my stuff."

It was pretty clear that Michael felt just as awkward about the whole scenario as I did. The rest of the group just kind of smiled and chuckled a bit, amused at our discomfort.

Patty then told me that they would figure out what time they would pick me up and let me know on Friday. I took that as my cue to leave them and went and got my things for lunch.

I filled Liz, Hope and Kristen in on what had transpired.

"Wow—you are lucky! I can't believe you are going," said Liz. She sounded happy for me, but I could tell she probably wished that she was going too.

"Thanks. I am pretty nervous about it, but it will be okay. So, what do you guys want to do?" I said trying to change the subject. We wound up landing on having a contest to see who could balance the farthest across the length of the curb without falling off. Not exactly dodgeball level of fun, but at least it was a challenge.

The rest of the week went by painstakingly slow. I avoided all eye contact with Michael. It was just too embarrassing to think about the fact that we would eventually have a couples' skate together. *I would have to hold his hand!* It was too much for either of us to verbalize. Instead, we did the opposite and completely ignored each other's existence.

I managed to avoid the topic with my friends at lunch and after a couple of days, I think they even forgot that I was going. Patty hadn't talked to me in class since the day I had to tell Michael that I could go, so it was easy to pretend that all was normal.

My biggest challenge was that my mind kept racing all over the place. I just couldn't picture where we were going and what it would be like. *How would "couples' skate" go? Would it be announced? Would we have to line up awkwardly?* These were all things I was desperate to know, but not able to ask because: 1) I wasn't really friends with Patty and 2) even if we were friends, I feel like she would laugh at me if I asked her because it wouldn't be cool.

Friday afternoon finally arrived, and I just about long jumped out of the bus. My Mom and I talked about what I should wear the next day. She didn't know what *Gloria Vanderbilt* jeans were either and, even if she did, she wasn't about to go running out to buy me some. My parents bought us new clothes before school, at Christmas and our birthdays. Rarely would an item be purchased other times unless there was a legitimate reason for doing so. So, thinking over what I had as options in my closet, I landed on the nicer of my two pairs of jeans, and a pink sweater that had a tiny blue embroidered heart shape at the center. It wasn't what I would call a "cool" outfit, but it was nice and pretty.

"Mom, do you think two French braids would look good?" I asked.

"Oh, yes. I think that would be beautiful."

"Could you do them for me tomorrow?

"It would be my pleasure, hon."

I laid my things out on my dresser. It was now 4:30 p.m. on Friday. I was going to get picked up by Patty's mom at 12:40 p.m. the next day. So, I just had to occupy myself until then. *Torture!*

My sister and I played *Uno* until my Dad came home with a pizza. We ate, took baths and got in our PJs. Normally, Friday night with my family was just about my favorite—the start of the weekend and no school. This Friday night, however, was just about going through the motions. We watched *The Dukes of Hazzard* and *Dallas*, as we always did—buttered popcorn and all—but it wasn't any fun.

I couldn't wait to fall asleep and get to the next day. It probably took me about an hour, maybe two, to fall asleep, but I eventually did.

Waking the next day, I sprung out of bed with excitement and headed downstairs. I was the first one downstairs—which was usual. I grabbed the leftover popcorn from the night before and made myself some chocolate milk—my Saturday morning treat.

Eventually Lala ambled downstairs and curled up with me to watch the Saturday morning line up of cartoons. Instead of lingering there until lunch like I normally did, I finished my morning snack and popped up to grab a pencil and paper to begin making myself a timeline for the day. My reasonable allotment of grooming and eating was as follows:

8-10	eat pancakes/finish cartoons
10-11	bath
11-11:30	change and blow dry hair
11:30-12:30	do hair
12:40	leave

Yesterday, when I saw Taryn arrive at school, I figured I had a few minutes before Patty's bus would come and I could ask her a few questions. Taryn was very sweet—especially when she didn't have to worry about looking uncool in front of Patty. She told me that there would be   food to buy at the Starflyer and that they all usually got a "*Tombstone*" pizza at some point. So, knowing this, I didn't factor any lunch into my schedule for the morning. Also, I usually had about seven or eight of my Dad's great pancakes, so I wasn't very hungry for lunch on Saturdays anyway.

Taryn also told me that you needed five dollars which covered admission and skate rentals. My parents planned to give me ten dollars, so that meant I would have five dollars for food. This was a big deal because usually I had to use my allowance to get anything on my own.

I followed my timeline exactly. The only problem was that it only took my Mom twenty minutes to do my hair, so I was ready to go at 11:50. Both my Mom and Dad said I looked very pretty. I really hated being described as "pretty." It sounded so boring and plain. I wanted to look "gorgeous" or "beautiful," but I had to admit, "pretty" was as good as I could get—I couldn't really fault them. There wasn't anything that made me stand out—not like Taryn's spectacular blue eyes fringed by insanely thick and pointy eyelashes or Patty's super blonde hair that was styled perfectly.

I kept checking in the mirror to see what I looked like. *The hair was good.* It looked a little youngish—but I really didn't know what else to do with it. I didn't wear makeup or lip gloss yet, so my face just looked how it always did.

I spent the next fifty minutes in a triangle between the door, the hall mirror, and the living room chair. I didn't stay in one spot for more than a minute or so and I think I was driving my mother crazy because she said, "Goodness! I wish they would just get here already before you wear a hole in our floor!"

Just then, I saw a very fancy looking car approach our driveway and pull in. "They're here! Bye!" I shouted. I scooted out the door, but both of my parents followed and introduced themselves to Patty's mother—Donna LaChance. She was very elegant looking—a bit older than my parents—but still, she was almost regal. Her short blondish hair was swept back from her face and she had dark eye makeup which made her blue eyes stand out underneath her stylish gold glasses. Gigantic diamond earrings completed the look.

Patty was in the front next to her Mom, and lowered the automatic glass window and said, "Hey!" then she giggled-snorted and motioned for me to get in the seat behind her.

"Hi! I'm Jenny—thanks for driving me," I said. To which, Patty rolled her eyes. *Was that too polite?*

"Hi dear, so nice to have your family at St. Liborius," purred Mrs. LaChance.

"Thanks. It has been really nice so far," I replied, fastening my seat belt.

"We're going to get Taryn now," stated Patty. We pulled out of the driveway and I gave a slight inconspicuous wave to try and put an end to my parent's exuberant goodbye—they looked like they were flapping birds about to take off, they were waving so hard.

Patty pressed a button that said "scan" to find a radio song she liked. She settled on *Land Down Under* from the band, Men at Work. It was a cool song for a cool girl in the fanciest car I had ever been in. Everything was so soft, cushioned, quiet and automatic. Our family had to roll our windows down and press different clunky buttons to look for stations.

"I like your car," I said.

"Thanks, It's a *Lincoln Town Car.*"

"Oh, it's really nice."

We rode in silence for ten more uncomfortable minutes until we picked up Taryn. She lived in a split-level home in a newer development. It looked like a nice house. Taryn burst out of the door and went in the other side so that she was sitting right next to me. She gave me a big smile and I felt much more at ease.

"Hey Tar," Patty said flatly, shortening Taryn's name to her best-friend nickname. After that, we were off to the Starflyer.

After ten minutes of driving, we made our way onto a very busy road with lots of restaurants, businesses and banks. As we slowed down, I could see the Starflyer come into view. It was a big, gray, rectangular looking building—kind of ugly. It had a *huge* neon sign on the top with the Starflyer spelled out in pink neon with a star and swoosh around it. It looked extremely exciting.

"See you girls at four, okay?" asked Mrs. LaChance.

"Yup, bye," said Patty and we were off.

I followed them in, and we got in line at a window. The attendant collected our money and we were given an entrance and skate rental ticket.

Down the hall and through another set of doors, we gave our entrance ticket to the man as we walked inside. Immediately, I was hit with the smell of rug, sweat, feet and popcorn. It was great.

We walked to the skate rental line and got our skates—all a light brown color with orange wheels. Just about the ugliest combination you could think of. It didn't matter, though—we all had them. I still followed behind as we went to a locker area and sat down to switch into our skates.

Luckily, I had roller skated in my old neighborhood on the sidewalks, so at least I knew how. "Oh, hey—there are the guys," said Patty as she waved to the twins and Michael, who was following behind them.

We all waved, and they sat down to put on their skates too as Patty said, "See you out there!" We followed her to the rink opening and down a step as the DJ welcomed us to the Starflyer, moving right into the song we had just heard in the car, *Land Down Under*.

The three of us started to make our way around the first lap as more and more people stepped down onto the rink floor.

I noticed that Patty had on her *Gloria Vanderbilt* jeans which I now saw were very dark blue jeans—almost black—with yellow stitching down the sides. There was a small, yellow swan on the front right pocket and Gloria Vanderbilt was stitched in cursive on the back-right pocket. She had on a white fuzzy sweater with puffy sleeves. Her hair was perfectly curled back, she had on small gold stud earrings and makeup—black eyeliner, mascara and lip gloss. She looked way older than I did.

Taryn also had on *Gloria Vanderbilt* jeans and a white shirt that had purple hearts going down the sides of both sleeves. Her hair was very long, shiny and curled under at the bottom. She had a gold heart necklace on top of her shirt. She was somewhere in between Patty's ultra, cool girl look and my little girl look. My French braids felt so ridiculous. *Why did I think this would look good? Couldn't I have just worn my hair down and curled?*

The twins and Michael were on the other side of the rink trying to hurry up and catch us. Eventually after three laps, they whisked by us—hooting and hollering.

Michael gave me a little smile and I smiled back at him—somewhat relieved that I had made it to the day and feeling like I was going to survive it after all.

We proceeded skating around for the next few songs: *Abracadabra, Jack & Diane,* and *Eye of the Tiger;* with the girls staying together and the boys passing us and then trying to catch up again. Every few laps or so, David would switch around to backwards skating which looked pretty cool. There were some really good skaters that could fly around the corners and cross their legs back and forth, so they almost looked like they were scissors. I stuck with a very straightforward motion, just trying to keep my balance and not attract any attention.

After a while, Matt suggested we all go get some pizza, so we made our way over to the food area and ordered a few *Tombstone* pizzas. Now that I had finally calmed down, the smell of the sauce and cheese hit my nose and I was starving. We all ordered some pop and sat down in a big, huge plastic booth to wait for the pizza.

Matt shared with us that his older sister had curled David's hair so that it would feather better. "Shut up!" David fired back at his brother and punched him good-naturedly in the arm. "At least my hair looks good. Yours looks like *Shredded Wheat!*" to which Matt scowled jokingly and stuck out his tongue.

"So, Jenny, was there roller skating in Connecticut?" Michael asked.

"Well, kind of...people roller skated around my neighborhood, but I never went to a roller-skating rink before—I like it," I replied feeling finally not as shy.

"Yeah, we come here a lot. Probably two times a month...there's not much else to do," said David.

"Pizza's ready!" grinned Michael who had wandered over to the counter to check. He brought over one pizza and David went and got the other one.

The pizzas were half the size of a normal pizza, thin and had big air bubbles in them. I could have probably eaten a whole one just by myself, but we had to share the two mini-pizzas between six people. We all dug in and I couldn't help feeling overjoyed to be eating pizza together as a group—like I belonged.

After a while we peeled off when *Let it Whip* started playing. It was a hard song to ignore—you had to get up and move when you heard the rhythmic crack of the whip sound.

David pulled his comb out from his back pocket and combed his feathered hair on both sides. Matt nudged him in the side, "You and your hair!"

"Gotta look good for the ladies!" he replied with a mischievous smile.

After a few laps, the music stopped, and the DJ announced that it would be couples' skate. I was about twenty feet from one of the rink entrances and made a beeline for it. My arm pits started to sweat. *Why did I wear a sweater? I had to hide! I could not, under any circumstances, hold Mike Bucknell's hand and do a couples' skate. I just couldn't!*

I found a big pole and just lingered there out of sight while the slow and silky song, *Eye in the Sky,* started playing.

"Jenny—what are you doing?" accused Patty. *She found me! Ahhh!*

"Oh, just coming to get some water, I'm really hot," I lied, badly—as I had no water.

"Well, Mike is looking all over for you! He wants to skate with you. Come on!" she proclaimed.

This was awful. I was trapped! I had never felt this level of embarrassment before in my life. I did *not* want to skate with Michael, but I also didn't want Patty to think I was a baby. Also, I felt a little bad for Michael. He was a nice guy and I didn't want to hurt his feelings. Reluctantly, I followed Patty back to the rink where Michael was waiting for me.

She cruised by me and went back to holding hands and skating with Matt—looking completely comfortable.

"Hi. Sorry—I just wanted to get some water," I lied again.

"Do you want to skate with me, Jenny?" Michael

asked with the most pained expression. At that moment, my feelings of wanting him not to be sad outweighed my embarrassment.

"Yeah. I do. It's just, would it be okay if I put my sweater over my hand?" Somehow, I felt like if I didn't have to touch his skin, I could go through with it.

"Uh…sure," he replied, not knowing what to make of this odd request.

I pulled my too-hot light pink sweater over my right hand and he grabbed onto it. We skated like that for a torturous two minutes that felt more like two years. I didn't dare glance over at Michael because that would have just about killed me. At one point in the song, the lyrics were, *"I can read your mind….."* *Could Michael read my mind?* If he could, he knew I would be screaming, *Make this song end!!!!*

Mercifully, the song finally ran its course and he released my hand and I blurted out, "Thanks! Bye," and went skate-running back to my hiding spot by the pole.

Patty, of course, found me again and looked so excited to see my reaction. "How was it? Do you like him?" she inquired.

I felt like I was finally able to breathe again and, as Taryn glided over to join us admitted, "He's really nice. It's just, it was my first couples' skate and it was kind of weird." I knew Patty would not think this admission was cool, but I was a bit exhausted from worrying about what she thought and just gave an honest answer.

"I felt like that too," admitted Taryn sweetly, making me feel like less of a baby.

"So…you should like Mike," forced Patty. *Geez—she was pushy!*

"Yeah. Uh. I guess I like him," I said not knowing what else to say. I *did* like him. I thought he was really nice. But I wasn't sure what she was asking of me.

"Great! I'll tell him to ask you out!" she said, absolutely thrilled.

"Okay," I agreed without a clue of what "going out" meant. Just then, *Come on Eileen* started to play and Taryn squealed with excitement and we all went out to skate again—it was a great song.

After we finished giggling from trying to skate faster and faster to the rising tempo of the song, they announced a limbo contest. We lined up and made our way under the pole which got lower and lower each lap. Six rounds in, I awkwardly wobbled to the left and landed on my butt.

David was very good at "shooting the duck," a roller skating move where you bent one leg, put your whole body close to the ground and jutted the other leg straight out. If you did it correctly, you resembled a pointed finger. He was so good, he managed to come in second place—just barely losing out to a much older-looking boy with the beginnings of a mustache who won the contest and a free *Tombstone* pizza.

The horns from the song, *Goody Two Shoes* got us all riled up again and we began skating around, this time as one big group of boys and girls. I could finally look at Michael again now that we were in the safety of a big group. A small spark of excitement that he liked me started to take hold and I began to feel a little silly about being scared to skate with him before.

When the song ended, they announced the last couples' skate of the day, the syrupy ballad, *Up Where we Belong* starting to play. I was standing right by Michael, so there was no escaping this time. Strangely, I wasn't as scared.

He just came over to me and held out his hand. This time, I didn't pull my sweater over it and we started gliding to the music. Michael asked, "Did you have fun today?"

"Yeah. It was really fun. Probably the most fun I've had here so far."

"Cool," Michael declared with a big grin. I liked that he really wasn't afraid to say what he was thinking and didn't seem to be overly worried about impressing Patty.

As the song ended and we moved towards the step, Michael turned to me and said, "Jenny, do you want to go out with me?"

I started to feel my face get hot again. "Ummm…where?"

"No," he laughed, "not to like, a place. Just, going out."

"Ohhhh! Um, okay!" I still wasn't one hundred percent sure what that meant—but I was guessing it meant we were kind of boyfriend-girlfriend. I wasn't sure of that. Still, I did think I liked him, so I felt somewhat okay with the fact that I told him yes.

"Good! Okay. Bye." Mike bolted away after that. I had the feeling he was waiting to ask me that for a while and was relieved to have gotten it over with. That made me like him even more.

The DJ announced the last song of the afternoon, *Hot in the City*. In a big pack again, our group started out with gusto but bit by bit, we lost energy and began peeling out of the rink one by one. When it was over, we went back to put on our shoes and wait to be picked up.

Michael's mom walked into the skating rink, a very tall and pretty lady with short brown, stylishly curled brown hair, and big blue eyes—just like Michael's. She waved to us girls and gathered up the boys and headed out.

Mrs. LaChance was soon to follow, and we all plopped into the *Lincoln Town Car*, completely exhausted.

"So, are you and Mike going out?" Patty turned to ask when the car started moving.

"Um, yeah."

"That's *so* good. He's such a nice kid. You'll make a great couple," Patty stated.

"That's great, Jenny! So cool." Taryn smiled enthusiastically.

"Thanks" I said—finally understanding that Michael and I were somewhat "a couple" now.

When we pulled into my driveway, I thanked Mrs. LaChance for driving me and said goodbye to Patty. I didn't really know if this day would mean we were now friends at school, but I was too tired to think any more about it.

My Mom opened the door and waved a thank you to Mrs. LaChance and turned to me eager to hear how it went. "So…how was it?"

"It was really fun, Mom. But now I am sooooo tired."

"Well, we are having steak sandwiches and chips tonight—so why don't you go run and take a shower before dinner so you can just relax." She smiled and thoughtfully didn't push for more details.

"Okay," I smiled and headed upstairs with a contented happiness that I was going eat one of my favorite dinners after the most fun day I'd had since moving.

THE FALCONS

A few weeks had passed since the big Starflyer outing and I found myself in an awkward pattern of not knowing how to balance my friendship with Liz, Hope and Kristen—the first friends I made at school— with my new "Starflyer" friends.

For the most part, I still found Liz, Hope and Kristen before school, had lunch with them and talked with them at recess. Every so often, however, Patty would summon me over with a question. Usually it had to do with reporting to her about what the latest news was with me and Michael. My reply was always pretty much the same—a very stutter-ish reply of, "Oh good. I think."

The truth was that nothing had really changed after we were officially "going out." We still barely talked to each other on the bus or anywhere else—so there wasn't a whole lot to report.

Patty would just kind of roll her eyes at me followed with her confident laugh that ended with a honk.

After the inquires, I would return to Liz, Hope and Kristen, and they would look at me with sympathy—as we all were a bit terrified of Patty. They knew it would have been a nerve-wracking exchange.

"What does she want to know?" Liz would ask from time to time.

"I dunno—she keeps asking me about Michael, but I don't know what she wants me to tell her because nothing really has changed." I had told Liz that I was now going out with Michael and she seemed impressed.

Liz told me that Patty had been going out with Matt since fourth grade and that sometimes they would hold hands under the table during special reading group. I didn't know anyone who was "going out" back in Connecticut, so this was all new territory. It seemed so grown up—part of me was excited by it all but the other part just wanted to go play *Barbies* with my sister.

I could tell that Liz was starting to get a little miffed with how frequently I was being called over by Patty, but she also knew that there was not much I could do about it. If Liz was summoned over by Patty—she would go. But Liz also knew that after all the years of knowing Patty, she was not going to be selected as a friend. Somehow, the knowledge that she was already rejected by Patty and that I was being tested out as a potential friend, made it tense between us.

Another change was that, occasionally, one of our classmates, John Arnold, would ask me to come join the boys during kickball at recess. John Arnold was a quiet boy that kept mostly to himself—but when it came to sports, he was a different person all together. I think he probably blocked out everything Mrs. Transki said during the day (his grades were mediocre at best, as I discovered when I was the "paper passer") and instead dreamed only of recess and catching balls.

During our gym time over the last few weeks, John would nod his head in approval when I would catch a ball or kick it respectably far. Since there was often an odd number of boys playing kickball at recess, John had begun to come over and ask me if I would join his team. (He and Matt were usually captains of each side since they were the strongest athletes.)

Enthusiastically I would say yes whenever he asked. In Connecticut, I loved playing on the softball team. In fact, I really loved playing any sport there was and found it way more exciting than just standing around in a circle talking about how much we hated homework.

The boys wouldn't play kickball every day, sometimes it was softball, sometimes races, sometimes they just shot at the basketball hoop or played jacks, but the days they needed an extra person, I would leave Liz, Hope and Kristen at recess.

Those were my favorite days—I felt so much like myself when I could just run around and show that I could play with the rest of them. There was a respect that I got from the boys when they knew I could kick it just about as far as any of them. This made me prouder than anything—much better than getting an A on a test or looking pretty.

After a few weeks of being included in kickball, Patty came up to me after recess and said, "Hey Jenny—what's with playing kickball?" Then she did one of her laughs that instantly made me feel like an idiot.

"I just like playing sports, I guess. It's fun," I replied honestly.

"Well, boys don't really like girls that are all sweaty, you know."

"Um…well I guess I *am* a little sweaty. But I can't help myself—I really like it."

"Michael and sweaty Jenny. Ha—what a pair! Do you think he likes it?"

"Well, I hadn't really thought about it. I don't know what he thinks."

"I'll ask him and let you know. You know, cheerleading tryouts are coming up for basketball. We all cheerlead—you should try it. It's not as…sweaty." To which Patty cackled and left me standing there feeling annoyed and humiliated at the same time.

I didn't really want her to ask Michael what he thought. The truth was I didn't really care—if he didn't like me for who I was, well, then I didn't really want to go out with him. Patty was scary—but she wasn't going to make me stop playing with the boys at recess, it was too much fun.

What was wrong with this place? They didn't seem to have many sports for girls—or girls that were interested in playing them. But I had to admit that the idea of cheerleading for St. Liborius DID seem kind of fun too. I had finished with the junior football cheerleading team and thankfully that meant I didn't have to see my crazy neighbor, Jennifer, on a regular basis. It was starting to get cold outside, so I didn't risk seeing her outside in her backyard either.

Liz told me that pretty much all the girls in the class were cheerleaders for the boys' basketball team at St. Liborius—she was too. Kristen was also a cheerleader, but Hope had asthma, so she stayed away.

Tryouts were going to be the following week and if I was interested, I had to call Miss Becky and sign up. If Liz and Kristen were on the team—it would make it easy to spend time with them and Taryn and Patty too. I planned to ask my Mom that night.

"Well, let me get more information—how many games and how far. I am not sure I can be driving you every weekend. But maybe if we could carpool, it might work," my Mom thought out loud.

Luckily, the talk with Miss Becky went well. She told my Mom all about the "Falcons" cheerleading and that is was a wonderful way for the girls of the class to bond. The games were only once a weekend and since most of the girls were on the team, should be easy to find people to carpool with. She gave my Mom the information about tryouts and told her to have me wear shorts, a t-shirt and tennis shoes. (Everyone here called sneakers "tennis shoes" which was strange because no one played tennis.)

The night of tryouts, we carpooled with Liz to the Mt. Carmel school gymnasium which was twenty minutes away—our own gym/cafeteria/auditorium was almost always being used for things like bridge groups or Rotary club—so we never did any afterschool activities there.

"I am so nervous! I feel like I want to throw up!" I told Liz.

"I am nervous too. They took almost all of us last year because it was just fourth grade basketball, but this year, fifth and sixth grade girls are combined and there are only twelve spots. Patty and Taryn will definitely make it—they are the best at it."

"How did tryouts work last time?"

"Uh, they just taught us two cheers and then we had to come in by ourselves and perform it in front of a table of a few judges."

"Oh my gosh—I'm going to die," I lamented.

We rode the rest of the way in silence. When we finally arrived, Mrs. Crispin walked us in and signed us up. She gave us a little encouraging wave and thumbs up sign and left to go back home.

Kristen, Patty, Shelly, Jenny T. and Taryn were already there, along with several girls from the sixth grade class that I slightly recognized but didn't know their names.

"Alright, Alright girls, come on over," Miss Becky said in a firm but sweet voice.

Miss Becky said she would be the Falcons JV cheerleading coach this year and that she was a college cheerleader at Iowa State University. She had beautiful blonde hair that was expertly feathered away from her face and big blue eyes with lots of eyeliner and mascara that made them pop.

She explained that she would be teaching us two cheers and then she would give us some time to practice them and then we would have to come in, one by one, and perform both cheers. It was just as Liz said. It didn't seem so bad—but the thought of coming in all alone was enough to make me want to vomit.

"Girls, you need to have crisp movements. Crisp! No chicken arms!" explained Miss Becky. "Your elbows should always be parallel with the shoulders and every clap should be held for a count of one before you release, got it?" We all nodded paying close attention.

"Also, girls you MUST smile, make eye contact, and nod your head briskly from time to time. Watch." She demonstrated this head nod, and which looked as if someone said, "Do you want some ice cream?" and she was signaling a very enthusiastic "Yes" by nodding her head curtly.

She taught us two cheers— "We're number one not two, not three, not four" and "R, E, B, O, U, N, D—rebound." For both cheers, she told us we needed to begin by saying, "Ready? Okay!" (Thankfully, I had mastered that part from the junior varsity football cheerleading.) Both cheers had routines to perform with kicks and claps and arm movements.

After about twenty minutes doing it together, we practiced for ten more minutes on our own and then we were all ushered out in the hall to wait for our turns to individually try out.

The sixth grade girls were called in first. The rest of us just stood around and kept talking about how nervous we were. Taryn was the first from our grade to be called in. She came out saying to Patty, "I think I did okay." Patty went in next. When she came out, her entire face was beet red. It seemed impossible to me that Patty was capable of being nervous—but there was the proof—her face told the truth—even Patty was human. She blurted out, "Oh my God,

Tar—that was horrible." They both went and sat down against the wall.

Kristen went next, followed by Liz. She came out and shrugged her shoulders as if to say, "We'll see!"

Then I heard my name called and went to the door like I was in a trance. My face got hot and I quickly went out in front of the table. Miss Becky said, "Go ahead Jenny whenever you are ready."

I remembered to say, "Ready? Okay" and then launched into the first cheer—which I think I did about five times faster than how Miss Becky showed us because I just wanted it to be over.

"Okay, hon, a little slower for the second cheer, okay?" said Miss Becky with a big sympathetic smile.

I managed to slow down my pace for the next cheer, but half-way through, couldn't remember what arm movement to do to the part where I was supposed to kneel with one leg and say in a very low voice, "RE-bound." I just pushed my arm to the side and hoped that was close. I finished up the cheer, said a quick "thank you" and practically ran out of the room.

Oh—that was awful! There's no chance I will make it.

Those of us that had finished, made our way to the walls and sat down. After about ten more minutes, we were called into the room.

"Well, you all did such a great job," said Miss Becky. "I wish we could keep you all, but we only have twelve uniforms and the routines are all based off of having twelve girls. If you didn't make it today, keep trying and come give it a go again next year, okay?" I instantly felt like she was talking to me and was already starting to mentally practice my "that's okay that I didn't make it" face.

Miss Becky started to read the names, I heard Taryn's name called and then Patty's. And then, I heard her say Jenny Foster and I was in elated disbelief! *I made it!*

Kristen, Liz, and Shelly from our class also made the team too but Jenny T. did not, and she looked very upset. Several girls from the sixth grade class started to walk away after they didn't hear their names—tears streaming down their faces. I tried to keep from celebrating too much in front of them as I knew they must have felt horrible.

My Mom was in the lobby and Liz and I made a beeline for her. As soon as we were in the safety of the car, we started to go crazy. "Oh my gosh—I can't believe we made it! I did soooooo bad—I just can't believe it." We both excitedly recapped every agonizing moment for my Mom who seemed genuinely happy for us.

The following week, we had two cheerleading practices where we crammed in learning seven cheers well enough to perform them at the first basketball game.

Our first game was against St. Mike's—their uniforms were navy blue and white. Our Falcon uniforms were light blue, white and yellow. I thought it was an unfortunate color combination and it didn't make any sense because our school uniforms were red—but even though it was a little ugly, it was still fun to wear. And when you added the saddle shoes and pom poms to the mix—it was downright exciting. I put in my usual barrettes and then had my Mom pull the rest of my hair into a ponytail. Miss Becky had given us all white and light blue ribbons to put in our hair, so my Mom fastened them into a bow over my ponytail.

When we walked into the first game at St. Mike's, you could hear buzzers and sneakers making screeching sounds. Then came the smell of rubber, sweat and popcorn. I could see a little gathering of a few cheerleaders who were already there in the hall. We waited for the other game to finish and then it would be our turn.

Patty and Taryn came in together and Taryn gave me her usual big smile. Patty said, "Hey guys. I am sooooo nervous. I am going to mess up, I know it."

"Uh-me too! We didn't have a long time to learn our routines," I lamented.

Then the final buzzer sounded and all the people from the previous game filed out and we made our way to the corner by the side of the bleachers. Miss Becky greeted us there.

"You girls are going to do great. I am going to have Patty call the cheers today, Okay?" That meant that Patty would pick what cheer we were going to do and then in a loud, deep voice she would say, "READY?" and we would shout, "OKAY!"

Miss Becky explained that we would rotate the cheers we knew and that, for this first game, we would go out at half time to the center of the court and do the "Blue and Gold" cheer. This was the longest and most complicated cheer, so it made sense that would be used at half time.

As the game started, we got all lined up in the corner—six girls were on one side of the corner and six on the other—so that we looked like a "L." My Mom stayed to watch the game and sat with Taryn's mom.

When the buzzer sounded, all the boys on our Falcon team came out on the court to be introduced. From our class, there was Gregg, Matt, David, Michael, Mark and John Arnold. When I was cheerleading for the town football team, it was okay—but now that I knew half of the boys on the team and they were from my school, I felt a wave of pride and excitement.

As the game went on, every cheer seemed

necessary to keep the spirits up for our team. I desperately wanted to win against St. Mike's. John Arnold turned out to be the best on the team, followed by David and Matt.

At halftime, we were up by four points. The boys cleared the court and huddled together to discuss what they would adjust for the second half. It was our turn! Patty looked at us with an expression that seemed to say: O*h my gosh-we have to go out in front of all those people now!* There was no stopping now. With a deep breath, I cartwheeled and jumped out to the center of the court with the rest of the girls.

We got in our spots and Patty called out, "Ready?"

And we shouted back with our biggest smiles, "Okay!'

"Blue and Go-old. Blue and Go-old. Don't mess with the best, cause the best don't mess! Don't fool with the cool, cause the cool don't fool!" we shouted while we clapped and stamped our feet to the rhythm. Then, repeated the verse again. At the very end, of the cheer, we attempted a very basic pyramid where Lisa and Angela from sixth grade were kneeling and Kristen kneeled on top of them (since she was the smallest.) Then Liz and I both stood to the side of the kneeling girls and each put one leg resting on their shoulders. Everyone else did the splits in front or to the side of us. It wasn't the most sophisticated pyramid, but it still probably looked okay from the bleachers, I'd imagined.

After the audience gave us a nice applause, we jumped and cartwheeled our way back over to the side. We all started hugging each other and laughing as we were so relieved to have completed our first half-time routine without any mistakes.

Miss Becky told us we did a great job and that we had a few minutes to use the bathrooms and grab some water if we wanted. Liz and I went out to the hallway and stood in the water fountain line.

Michael came up and stood right behind me. "Hi Jenny. You guys are doing a great job." Michael's face looked flushed from running and his hair was really sweaty—but he still looked cute. I was pretty happy to see him.

"Thanks!" I said, marveling at how I was starting to feel more comfortable talking to him even though we were "going out."

"I hope you guys win! You're all playing so good."

"Thanks," he replied. "My jump shot is kinda stinky right now, but oh well."

I couldn't think of anything else to say, so I was relieved when the person in front of me finished. I turned and sipped the water for a couple of seconds wishing I could gulp down water for a good minute— I was so thirsty! With Michael waiting behind me, though, I felt too self-conscious to drink for long, so

I stopped and wished him good luck in the second half.

I saw my Mom as we were walking back to our corner and she gave me a wave and mouthed "You're doing great."

The rest of the game continued with St. Mike's and St. Liborius trading leads—we would go up by a few, and then they would gain momentum and steal the lead back. At the quarter, St. Mike's was in the lead by five points and we started getting worried we wouldn't be able to turn it around again.

We heard the St. Mike's cheerleaders start the "Spirit" cheer where they would say, "We've got spirit, yes we do! We've got spirit, how about you?"

To which we would yell back louder the same phrase to them across the auditorium. This continued a few times until St. Mike's roared back, "We've got more! We've got more!"

We would finish the cheer war with, "We've got it ALL! We've got it ALL!"

Then, both cheerleading corners would go quiet—temporarily out of breath from yelling as hard as we could.

Our Falcon boys seemed to get a little pep in their step and all the sudden got a shot and then stole the ball away to get another quick two points. Now they were chasing the lead by only one point.

There was only thirty seconds left on the clock and St. Mike's was taking their time bringing the ball down to their side of the court—hoping to use up the remaining time on the clock so we wouldn't have a chance to get another basket.

Their forward, who was tiny but amazing at handling the ball, suddenly burst by David who was defending him and went in for the layup. Michael was ready in his defensive position and, as their forward went up for the shot, he blocked it perfectly and the ball fell into the hands of John Arnold.

John sprinted down to our side and, with only ten seconds left on the clock, went for a layup. He was going a little too fast, though, and his shot bounced off the backboard. Matt Rubinski grabbed the rebound and St. Mike's tried to block his shot by fouling him. The shot didn't go in, but with three seconds left on the clock, the referee signaled that we had two foul shot attempts.

We were all going wild as the teams lined up for the free throws. A hush then fell over the auditorium as Matt bounced the ball three times, took a big puffy breath out, looked at the basket, bounced the ball two more times, took one more breath and then launched the first shot. It went in without hitting anything, but the net and our side of the auditorium erupted like a volcano. *Tie game!* If he missed the second shot, at least we had a chance to go into overtime.

The auditorium quieted once more—the air electric with anticipation. Liz, Taryn and I were holding hands. Matt went through the same routine—three bounces, breath, look at the basket, two bounces, breath, and shot. We all held our breath as the ball soared toward the backboard and fell to the left side of the rim making a little ding sound, then bounced gently over to the right rim and, finally, fell into the basket to an explosion of cheers. We were all jumping up hugging each other in a big circle.

The referee blew the whistle and handed the ball to St. Mike's. They would have one more chance to try and get the ball down the court for a shot. The whistle sounded again and their point guard threw the ball in to his teammate who launched the ball into the air desperately towards the basket. The ball fell about twenty feet short as the buzzer sounded. The Falcon fans erupted again and continued to jump up and down and hug each other—all sharing in the victory.

After a couple of minutes of laughing and recounting moments of the game, my Mom came over from the bleachers and motioned towards the door.

We headed home and my head was humming with the thrill of the win and excitement at having been a part of it and feeling like I belonged. I thought back to last year when I was a fourth grader in Connecticut and couldn't believe how much older I felt now. *I was a cheerleader at my OWN school, cheering for the boys in my class and my "kind of" boyfriend.* It seemed hard to believe.

CHRISTMAS

"Nooooo! We're not going home for Christmas?" I wailed. Every Christmas, our family would spend the school vacation with our Drexel Hill relatives.

My grandparents lived about a half of a mile from each other, so if we slept at my Mema's house (my Dad's mom) it was just a walk up the street to see Ganny and D-Dad (my mom's parents.) My Baba died when I was much younger and we always tried to stay with Mema because she was alone.

"I know, Jenny. We want to go too—but it's too far to drive this time of year. We don't know if it will snow and it's just too dangerous to drive seventeen hours across the country in the winter. We will go this summer, okay?" reasoned my Mom. My Dad just looked at me with an expression of heartache for causing such disappointment.

I nodded that I understood, which I supposed I did, but it seemed way too sad to think about. *I wouldn't get to see all of my relatives. I loved them all so much!* Since we had moved so often, Drexel Hill had always been home to me—the place we always came back to and that had all my sweet grandparents, aunts, uncles and cousins. Drexel Hill Pizza was my favorite pizza—all crunchy crust and gooey cheese and I could almost taste the crackle of the chocolate coating from the *Dilly Bars* at *Dairy Queen* that my D-Dad would get for us after dinner.

I had a ton of relatives—my Mom had two brothers and four sisters. My Dad had a brother and two sisters. I had eighteen cousins—my closest was just one year older than me, Elisa. Elisa and I always had sleepovers when my family would stay in Drexel Hill. We would order cheesesteaks and eat ice pops— our favorite. Then, we'd sit in her double bed and talk all day and into the night (mostly about her life because it was way more exciting than mine—her being a year older and all.)

I would not get to go to the movies and the mall which was called the *"Bazaar"* (which I always found to be a strange and unappealing name for a mall) with my Aunt Ellie. There would be no sleepovers at my godmother, Aunt Karen's house, where I could eat *Jiffy Pop* and stay up way past my bedtime watching ABC's *Movie of the Week*. My Ganny's bed, all warm and toasty from her electric blanket, would have to wait. We would have to save the crosswords puzzles and *Family Feud* watching until the summer.

What hurt most to think about was not spending New Year's Eve with my Mema while we watched

Dick Clark's Rockin' Eve, drank root beer and ate cheese doodles and peanuts on the TV trays. I had done that every year—my parents, dressed all fancy, off to their mysterious adult parties. I never actually made it to midnight, but I loved laughing with my Mema and having her sing *Take Me Out to the Ball Game* and *Tora Lora Lora* before I fell asleep.

I didn't even know what to look forward to now. *What would we do for the whole week after Christmas?* It didn't seem like much fun just staying here in the freezing cold with nothing to do—and with just our family. I went up to my room, grabbed Popcorn and cried deeply into my pillow.

There was one last week of school before Christmas vacation started and all I could think about was having a break from homework and the cooped-up classroom. It seemed like every week was so long now. The cold weather had kept us from recess over the last few weeks. It had been between twenty and thirty degrees out, but with the "wind-chill factor," it often felt like below zero.

Wind-chill factor was a new experience for me. It often felt thirty or forty degrees colder than the actual temperature because the winds whipped so fiercely. I had never endured such an intense cold in my life.

We usually stayed inside for recess and played *Connect Four* or *Uno.* Sometimes, we would make get well cards for a parishioner that wasn't well.

This week, our class was in charge of the school mass which meant that we were able to pick out the songs, readers, and gift bearers. David always wanted to pick *Kumbaya*. It was his favorite church song and made him happy. Since we all liked when David was happy—his face would get in the biggest, crinkly smile—we all agreed.

I was picked to be one of the gift bearers, along with Matt and Taryn.

When Friday came and it was time to bring up the gifts, I suddenly got nervous. I had brought up the gifts a long time ago when we were in Connecticut, but it was a Sunday mass and I didn't know most of the people. This time, our entire school would be looking at us.

During the Prayer of the Faithful, Mrs. Transki gave us a nod and we walked to the back of the church and picked up the wine and hosts. We knew to wait for the song to walk back up.

Once the song started, Matt handed Taryn and me a dish with the unblessed communion hosts. He held the wine and we started to move up the aisle in a slow step together, pause, step together rhythm. The younger grades seated in the back did not pay attention to us as we went by, but as we got to where the fifth, sixth, seventh and eighth graders were sitting, more heads looked at us in curiosity. Out of the corner of my eye, I saw Sherri from eighth grade (the girl who had called me a sunflower on the first day) scrunch her face up in a mocking expression and point at us laughing.

My head got completely hot and I looked down and directly in front of me. *Just don't drop it!* Michael and Mark were altar boys today and, as we reached Father Doyle, he took the dish from me and handed it to Michael. *Phew, I made it!* Michael looked right at me and smiled. I couldn't help but smile back— slightly biting my lip. He then took the dish from Taryn and handed it to Mark. When he last took the wine from Matt, we all did a small bow, as we had been instructed, and walked back to our seats. It took me a full ten minutes before I felt the flush of embarrassment subside.

As we were walking back over from the church to the school, Michael caught up to me and said, "Hey, Jenny, will you be home after school today?"

We never really had much going on Friday nights except the usual pizza and family TV watching, so I said, "Yeah—I'll just be home."

"Great! I just have something I want to give you and my Mom was gonna drop me by before basketball practice. Is that okay?"

"Yeah. Sure!" I said. *What was he going to give me?*

"Good. Okay, I should be there around 4:15. See you later." Then Michael ran and caught up to the boys.

The rest of the afternoon thankfully went by quickly. We had a small class Christmas party. Taryn and Mark's parents had brought in cupcakes. We were given a Christmas tree napkin and each got to pick either a vanilla cupcake with vanilla icing and rainbow sprinkles or a chocolate cupcake with chocolate icing and *M&M's*. I went for chocolate.

Mrs. Transki put on the *Beach Boys Christmas* album while we ate our cupcakes. Then we cleaned up and played "Head's Up, Seven Up." This was one of my favorite classroom games of all time—seven students stood at the front of the room and the rest of the class had to put their heads down, one arm further covering the face and the other, bent at a 90 degree angle with the thumb sticking up in the air. When the teacher would signal, the "Seven Up," students would go around the room and each put down the thumb of one classmate and go back up to the front of the room. When all the "Sevens" were back up to the front of the room, Mrs. Transki would say, "Head's Up, Seven Up."

The students whose thumbs were pressed down would also stand up. One at a time, the guessers would try to pick who pressed their thumb down. If they guessed correctly, they would take the place of one of the "Seven." If they guessed incorrectly, they would have to sit back down. It helped to guess towards the end, as the possibilities narrowed down considerably.

On our first go-around, I guessed Michael. I was wrong. *Embarrassing!* The second time, I picked Shelly, and was wrong again. The third time, with only the choice of Scott or David left standing, I guessed David and was right.

When it was my turn to press down a thumb, I pressed down Liz's—I was too shy to press down a boy's thumb.

Liz guessed me right away. And then the game was over.

The finale to our classroom celebration was giving out our "Secret Santa" gift. I had picked Shelly a couple of weeks ago. We were to keep our present to no more than five dollars. I bought her a few sheets of puffy rainbow stickers (she had one of the best sticker collections in our class) and small ribbons to make ribbon barrettes.

"Thanks Jenny, I LOVE it!" said Shelly in her gentle voice. She truly seemed happy and started gracefully putting her stickers in her sticker book right away.

Hope came up quietly next to me and shyly handed me a small present. I pulled off the red bow and tore open the green and white striped wrapping paper to reveal a Judy Blume book titled *Blubber.*

"It's about a girl in fifth grade and she is from

Pennsylvania!" said Hope excitedly with her round eyes filled with joy. "That's where you were born, right?"

"It is! Thanks so much, Hope! I really like Judy Blume books. It will be fun to read over vacation. Thank you!" I gave Hope a hug—touched that she remembered that I was from Pennsylvania and was so excited to give me this gift.

Later that afternoon, I jumped off the bus feeling relieved to be done with school for a while, excited for Christmas day, but still a little sad at not to be going to Drexel Hill. I got out of my uniform and into some jeans and a rainbow striped top.

"Well this is unusual that you are getting out of your uniform," remarked my Mom. Usually, I lazily stayed in my uniform until after dinner when I would take a bath.

"Oh, I just thought I'd get out of it. Oh, and Michael Bucknell said he needed to give me something before basketball practice?" I said this like it was a question and didn't really understand why he was coming over. "So, he is coming at 4:15 with his Mom."

"Ohhhhh—I see. Now I understand the outfit change." *Ugh! That woman knew everything! Was it that obvious that I was excited for him to come over?*

"No, Mom! I just wanted to get out of my uniform—it's kind of smelly!"

"Uh-huh," she muttered not buying my lie, which really annoyed me. She went upstairs—I imagined in order to brush her hair before Mrs. Bucknell got here.

Not long after, the doorbell rang, and my sister ran to the front door. "Hey! It's a weird guy! Weird guy here! Weird guy here!" she kept yelling like he was about to bust in and capture her.

"Lala—it's just Michael from my class. It's okay. Go back to *Scooby Doo*." Lala stayed right there despite my instruction, not going to miss out for a second.

I opened the door. Michael was standing there in his basketball shorts and a coat—calves exposed to the freezing cold. His Mom was sitting in the car which was still idling.

"Hi, do you want to come in?" I said feeling bad that he must be so cold.

"Come in! Come in! Come in," yelled Lala jumping up and down with her curly pigtails flying.

"Lala!" I yelled, embarrassed.

"That's okay. I have to go, I just wanted to give you this Christmas present. Merry Christmas, Jenny."

"Merry Christmas, Michael. I feel horrible! I didn't get you anything!" *Why didn't I think to get him anything?*

"That's okay. Okay, I've gotta go—you can open it later. Bye! See you when school is back." Michael blurted and waved as he ran back to the car. Mrs. Bucknell also gave me a small wave from inside the car.

I closed the door. "What is it? Open it! Open it!" squealed Lala. My Mom came down the stairs.

"Did he go already? I wanted to say hello," she said, disappointed.

"He had to go to practice," I said, completely relieved that she didn't have a chance of saying something completely embarrassing in front of him. "His Mom was waiting for him in the car."

"Are you going to open it now?" asked my Mom.

"Can I?" I asked.

"Sure!"

I started opening the little box which was wrapped in red paper with silver snowflakes. I pulled open the top of a box to reveal a little golden bracelet with a small light-blue bird in the middle.

"Oh, that is *so* pretty," exclaimed my Mom. "What a thoughtful gift."

"BIRDIE!" Lala gasped.

"Yeah, it's nice," I said, wanting the attention to stop. I went up to my room and put it on. *I think I have a boyfriend! And I think I just got my first present from a boyfriend!* I looked at my little birdie bracelet and smiled. *I was a girlfriend. Michael Bucknell's girlfriend.* It felt amazing. I got out my diary and, on the back page, practiced writing *Jennifer Bucknell* in cursive a few times.

On Christmas Eve a few days later, we finished our dinner of cube steak, mashed potatoes and peas and ran upstairs to get ready for bed.

The Muppet Movie was on that evening and we all planned to watch it. Normally, I would have been so excited to watch it—I loved *The Muppets*—but I already knew that I would be way too excited to enjoy the movie.

Halfway through the movie, I announced that I was going to bed.

"Night hon!" said my Mom giving me a kiss.

"Night, Nif. Good luck trying to fall asleep," my Dad said with a little sympathetic smile. He knew me so well.

I went over to give Lala a kiss but she kept bobbing her head away from my face so that she could see the movie. I gave her a little peck on her head and bounded upstairs—two steps at a time.

Snuggled in tight with Popcorn, I started to think about what my presents might be. I did that for about an hour—it was then 9:17 p.m.

My mind wandered all over the place while I tried the normal tricks of counting down from a hundred, imagining sheep jumping over the fence and saying the Our Father. A quick glance at "the bird" revealed it was then 9:53 p.m. *Oh—this was pure torture! This time, I will count sheep down from 200. 200 Sheep going over the fence. 199 Sheep going over the fence. 198 Sheep going over the fence....167 Sheep going over the fence....123 Sheep going over the fence....*

The next thing I knew "the bird" mercifully read 6:23 a.m. *Hooray! It was Christmas!* I jumped up, went to the bathroom and brushed my teeth. I then went into Lala's room and snuck under the covers with her.

"Huh....mmm...what?' Lala grumbled.

"It's Christmas, Lala! Wake up."

Her eyes suddenly got wide and she sat straight up. "It's Christmas! It's Christmas! It's Christmas!" she screamed as she darted up and began jumping up and down on the bed.

We ran into my parents' room and to their bed where they were just two lumps under the covers.

"Mom?" I whispered in her ear. "Mom? You awake? It's Christmas." It was never easy attempting to rouse my Mom.

"Hrrrm? Uhh…mmm," she mumbled and turned over, with no indication on having understood that it was Christmas and we were dying of anticipation.

"Daddy! Daaaaaaddddy! It's Christmas!" Lala had gotten on top of the lump that was my Dad and started jumping up and down.

"Uhhhh girls. What time is it?" breathed Mom, slowly coming to her senses.

"6:30 Mom!" I announced proudly. We weren't allowed to come in before 6:30 a.m., that was the rule.

"Okay, Okay. Give us a few minutes," said my Dad who slowly started showing signs of upward momentum. Eventually they made their way to the bathroom, brushed their teeth and put on their robes.

We all kneeled around the bed and said Happy Birthday to Jesus, held hands and prayed the Our Father together. We got up and my Mom went to go pull Kirk from his crib while my Dad went downstairs to see if Santa Claus had come. We had to sit on top of the stairs until he gave us the word.

Lala and I kept looking at each other, hugging and clapping our hands while we saw lights turn on downstairs and Elvis' voice sang, "*Here comes Santa Claus, Here comes Santa Claus, right down Santa Claus*

Lane..."

"Looks like Santa's been here!" Dad announced. "Come on down!" To which we responded by trampling down the stairs at a perilous speed, holding on to the railing for dear life.

We rounded the corner to a scene of present towers, a lit Christmas tree and the beginnings of a nice crackling fire in the fireplace.

My Mom came down after us holding Kirk who was clapping and saying, "Pres-ant. Pres-ant."

"Okay, Jennifer, your pile is on the couch and Lala you are on this chair," said Mom. She had explained to us a while back that she had written a note to Santa specifically requesting the areas she would like the presents grouped in, so that it would be less confusing. Apparently, Santa was usually very accommodating to parent's requests.

Before we went to our piles, however, we always gave our presents to each other first. Lala would have preferred to start tearing into her pile but, as the older sister, I made the rules.

We each handed out the presents we had bought at *Santa's Workshop* (a temporary store in the mall where children could buy presents for their families.)

I gave Lala some sparkly lip gloss, my brother a little red toy car, and my Mom a baking spoon that she seemed very surprised and delighted by. I was most excited to see my Dad's reaction to his present. I had found a paper weight that said "The Turd Bird" across the bottom. It was shaped like a poop with little feathers coming out here and there, legs, eyes and a beak. My Dad couldn't resist poop humor.

As predicted, he opened it and started to laugh. And this turned into a gasping laugh—my favorite kind. My Dad would hold one hand on the side of his face, with his eyes closed and then wrap his other arm across his stomach. He would start the gasp-laughing with a loud couple of noises that sounded like, "Kee! Kee!" and then he would fold over gasping for air. He would end it with an "Ahhhhh-boy." It was a great to watch.

Next, we made our way through the stockings filled with candy, soaps, crayons and nail polish. Then it was onto the piles. We all were an explosion of unwrapping and gasping. My Mom smiling and watching the fun while putting the discarded wrapping paper in trash bags. Lala would scream up and down for every single present. One time, I had asked her, "What is it?" to which she replied, "I don't know!" but that didn't make her any less excited. She really, really, really loved anything that was wrapped. It made us all smile to witness how happy she was.

I uncovered a few new sweaters, curlers, socks, a new stuffed animal dog, a pogo stick, a *Muppets Movie* album, a John Denver album, a *Barbie* Doll with straight, long white/blonde hair (*so pretty!*) and my absolutely favorite present—*Gloria Vanderbilt* jeans! I couldn't believe I was now the owner of a sleek new pair of *Gloria Vanderbilt* jeans. They looked so cool. I couldn't wait to wear them the next time I went roller-skating.

Eventually, we had breakfast and then got cleaned up and went to church. It was a great day.

The rest of the week felt like new territory—as we had never been "just us" for the week after Christmas. I had gotten over the fact that we wouldn't be seeing our relatives and was happy that we still could look forward to being with them in the summer. In the meantime, we did some fun things over the week which I noted in my diary so I could make sure to tell Karen in my next letter:

❀ New pizza place! My parent's new friends told us about this great pizza place—Sanfratello's. We got all dressed up and went there one night. It was a half hour drive from our house, and we passed by where Al Capone, the gangster, was from—Cicero. The building was an old house that had multiple levels. We waited forty minutes to be seated and then it took another forty-five minutes before our pizza came. We were all starving and my Mom kept asking the waitress for crackers to tide us over. It was all worth the wait because delivered to our table was the most unusual pizza I had ever seen! It was in a deep, pie-shaped pan with very thick dough with the cheese on the bottom and the sauce on top. It looked very strange to have the sauce on the top—but the taste was absolutely out of this world! I thought that if I had this pizza every day of my life, I wouldn't get bored—it was that good.

❀ I had a naming ceremony for my new stuffed animal dog. I lined up ALL my stuffed animals in order of importance—Popcorn as the head of ceremonies. After some talk, we decided on the name of "Sandy" for the new light brown golden retriever. Instantly, Sandy was a hit with all my stuffed-animal friends.

❀ My Dad took me with him to work one day. My duties were to open and sort mail at a desk in the middle of the office. As my reward, he brought me to *Chuck E. Cheese's* for lunch. It was neat to see where my Dad went during the day. He was the manager of an insurance office and I could tell people really liked him because they had big, genuine smiles on their faces when he would say hello. He told me on the drive in, that he was trying to get everyone to do a good job and have fun at the same time. He explained that you could always get your point across more effectively by making someone laugh. He also liked to hold contests to reach office goals and would take the winner out to lunch. He said the contests were working well—the mood of the office was getting much better and he loved learning more about people when he would go to lunch with them. It made me proud that my father tried so hard and that he was making people happier.

- We went to see the *Dark Crystal* at the movies—which was very scary. It was kind of like *The Muppets*—but scary Muppets! I had terrible nightmares that night that my face kept melting off and that Lala had turned into a zombie.

- Jennifer Barrow asked me to come over to play and I didn't want to but didn't know how to say no, so I went over. To my surprise, we actually had fun. We went in her basement to see her new hideout. It was the "crawlspace" which you got to by climbing through a square hole in the side of her basement, which opened to a half of a floor that was right under where her garage was. The floor of the crawlspace was all rocks and there was a light on the ceiling. She had put a small area rug on the rocks and there was a tape recorder, lamp and a typewriter. We crawled up into this new area and played secretary all afternoon while we listened to *Gloria* over and over again on her tape recorder.

- Lala and I had fun nights "sleeping out" in new spots. Sometimes, we would sleep out on the landing in the hallway—other times, we would put pillows on the floor in my room. We would take turn scratching each other's backs and singing songs. We also had one really fun afternoon where we set up a whole

Barbie town in her room. She had gotten the *Barbie Dream Townhouse* for Christmas—which had an elevator and three floors. We used hand towels to make beds at "campsites" around the *Barbie Dream Townhouse.* We used tissues to make the pillows and roads were created by lining up crayons on both sides. Grocery and clothes stores were represented by various sized present boxes. Most of the fun was in setting up this town. By the time we created it, we only imagined up a few *Barbie* scenarios of "coming over for coffee" and "shopping for a new dress" before we called it quits.

By the following Sunday night, I was looking forward to going back to school. I never got around to writing Karen. I just didn't feel like it and I was too excited to see my friends again and to have more basketball games to cheerlead for. I also hoped I would get to go to the Starflyer again, but no one had asked me to go since that first time. I imagined that Patty would be the one to decide when that would happen next—I would just have to wait.

SLEEPOVER AT PATTY'S

"Hey Jenny!" Michael waved as I got on the bus Monday morning.

"Hi," I replied and sat in the seat opposite of Michael—a bold move for me.

"How was vacation?"

"Pretty good…how 'bout you?"

"Great. I played *Atari* a lot. It was nice to lie around. What d'you do?"

"Um…lots a stuff. Let's see, I saw *Dark Crystal* and…"

"Me too!"

"You did? I hated it—I was so scared to go to sleep for days!"

Michael laughed at that. "I guess it was a little

creepy."

"Yes! And then you know, just kind of did stuff with my family."

"Yeah—me too. So, uh, I think Matt and David were talking about going to the Starflyer on Saturday. Our game this weekend is on Sunday—so we have the day free."

"Oh, fun."

'Yeah, I'm sure the other girls will be going, just ask Patty."

I didn't like the idea of approaching Patty about going. *What if I asked her and she just laughed at me? And why did Michael want me to ask her about it, like she was the boss? Why did everyone let her be in charge? He seemed too smart for that.*

"Okay…and thanks again for the bracelet, that was really nice."

"Oh, uh, yeah, you're welcome," Mike said—his face getting redder by the second. That awkwardly ended our conversation and we both stared out our windows until the bus got to school.

The week went by without much fanfare—it was almost like we never left school.

By Wednesday, Patty still hadn't mentioned anything about skating to me. Not that she really talked to me much—but she occasionally would look over my way and laugh whenever she thought someone said something stupid.

That night at cheerleading practice, however, she came over and asked me to sleepover on Friday. She said I could come over to her house around 5 p.m.—Taryn was coming too—and her Mom would bring us to the Starflyer the next day.

I couldn't believe it! Patty was inviting me over to her house! The idea of that much time in Patty's presence avoiding doing anything that she would make fun of was a little daunting. But I couldn't help feeling special—she picked *me* to come over! She was the most popular girl in my class, and she wanted to hang out with me! *Did that mean that I was popular now too?*

Gratefully, my parents said it was fine to sleepover and they would pick us girls up from the Starflyer on Saturday.

That Friday, I packed a bag with my rainbow PJs, (the least babyish ones I had) my new *Gloria Vanderbilt* jeans, a plain purple long sleeved shirt, socks, underwear, sneakers, a toothbrush, toothpaste, and a hairbrush. I contemplated packing Popcorn—I hadn't really ever gone away overnight anywhere and not brought him—but I was too afraid Patty would think I was a dork. So, Popcorn was left in charge of taking care of the other stuffed animals.

"Why are you so quiet, hon?" my Mom asked as she was driving me over.

"Huh? Oh, I dunno…I'm just a little nervous, I guess."

"Well, just be yourself, sweetie. You'll be fine."

"I know. It's just, you know, I'm weird and that's not cool sometimes."

"You're not *weird*!" she said—shocked that I would say that.

"No, Mom. I meant weird in a *good* way. Like how Dad is weird. It's just, you know, you need to feel safe to act like yourself. Patty doesn't get *weird*."

"Oh…well, if she doesn't like you for you, then she's not a good friend."

"I know. I know," I said, giving up.

My Mom didn't understand. Acting crazy around Liz or Jennifer Barrow was fine. But Patty would just raise her eyebrows at me if I did something she thought was uncool. I didn't want to care what she thought, and sometimes I was very good at feeling confident to just be "me," but I had to be honest that I still did desperately want to impress her. I wanted to try to be more grown up.

We pulled into a U-shaped driveway which led to a grand entrance of an elegant looking house. While it appeared to be only one level, it was impressively sprawled out—like a museum.

My Mom helped me out with my bag and we both stood dwarfed at the door, which was half glass, half wood. It had fancy, swirly patterns in the glass and guarding the side of them were two enormous urns with cork-screw shaped bushes towering out of them—almost like soft-serve ice cream cones.

I took a deep breath as my Mom pressed the doorbell which chimed a little tune of *Da-da, doh-doh. Doh-doh, da-da.* We looked at each other and then back straight ahead intimidated by the grandeur of it all.

After a few seconds, we heard laughing and running, and Patty opened the door with Taryn next to her.

"Hey! Come in," Patty breathlessly stated. Her mom coming up behind her.

"Hi Joan, hi Jenny, dear." Mrs. LaChance welcomed us warmly.

"Hi Donna. Thanks for having her over. So, I'll get them tomorrow and bring them back, right?" said my Mom, warmly back, but not wanting to linger.

"Sounds good. Have a good night—the girls will have a great time," she declared. I felt assured by her confidence that it would be true.

"Great. Have a good night, Jenny."

"Bye…see ya tomorrow," I blurted dismissively.

With that, Mrs. LaChance went back to the kitchen and Patty took me on a tour of the most impressive home I had ever been in. Each room seemed to be a different level. We stepped down into the foyer, but up into the dining room. Then down into the family room, but back up into her bedroom. Patty had a huge canopy bed, with a ruffled purple comforter and about ten pillows. The white carpet must have been two inches tall—it felt like a cloud. It was a princess fantasy room. All I could think was they must be super rich! I couldn't have imagined my Mom buying more than one pillow for our beds— that would be so expensive and silly. In Patty's home, endless pillows made perfect sense.

"Here, just put your stuff down—we'll come back later to sleep. Let's go make a routine in the basement," declared Patty.

"Yeah!" said Taryn, very excited to do a routine.

"Yeah!" I echoed, thrilled to be part of the fun.

We went through Patty's family room to the basement stairs which led to a series of four huge finished basement rooms—one leading into the next. The first room was some sort of office, the second room had a bar, the third room had a pool table, and a few stand up video games and the last room was like

145

another family room with a bunch of couches and a fluffy carpet.   Unlike the lofty heights upstairs, these rooms had low ceilings and it felt like you were in a secret underground fort.

Patty had a big boom box and a bunch of tapes in the family room. I didn't own tapes. I just had records. My Mom thought it was crazy to buy all the same music again, just so you could play it on a tape player. Clearly, Mrs. LaChance didn't give it a second thought.

We tried to make a routine to *Maneater* and then to *Billie Jean*—but finally found the right rhythm with *Puttin on the Ritz*. After an hour or so of twirls, front walkovers, and trying to keep a straight face while we shimmied towards each other to the tap-dancing part, we fell on the floor laughing and exhausted.

"Patty! Pizza's here!" boomed Patty's Mom's voice from the intercom system. She went up to hit the button to respond back.

"K…we're coming up," she gasped. I had never seen an intercom system before, and it made be silently giggle to picture one in our house. Somehow, I just couldn't imagine my Dad saying, "Niffer, your cereal is ready!"

Upstairs, Patty's mom had laid out a fifth grader's dream dinner—pizza, *Sprite*, *Coke*, french fries, and a basket full of *Hostess* cupcakes. We each grabbed a plate and I wasn't shy about piling on as much as I could.

We followed Patty to the upstairs family room, and we ate, plates on laps, while watching *Happy Days* on TV.

"You guys, after we eat, we should make generic awards!" said Patty.

"What are generic awards?" I asked, almost afraid to know.

"You know—like the poor brand. Like probably everything Shelly and Liz have." Then Patty let out one of her signature snorts.

"Okay," said Taryn, not sounding overly enthusiastic.

I felt a pit in my stomach. *How could I make fun of anyone just because they didn't have a lot of money to spend on things? Liz and Shelly were nice and it wasn't their fault they weren't rich like Patty.*

"Well, how about we pick generic things? Like the worst outfit on this show?" I tried.

"Uh, that's not what I mean. I think we should pick out someone each week, and we can just make a little award—we won't actually *give* it to them. We'll just say it to ourselves. It would be *so* funny. Like, did you see Shelly's new shoes? They are soooooo generic. I would die!"

"I know. They are really, really ugly," said Taryn,

laughing now with Patty. I was shocked. I thought Taryn was nicer than that. *Was she just saying that because she was afraid of Patty? Or was she mean sometimes too? How could I go along with this?*

Feeling more scared of Patty picking on me, I ignored my conscience, shrugged my shoulders and agreed.

Patty got up, put her plate on the counter and grabbed a paper and some markers. She then went on to write: Generic Award. 1983. January. 1st winner: Shelly. For: Ugly Shoes. Then she drew the green and black rectangles that I saw at Liz's house that signified the "generic brand."

"I'll keep them all here. So, our first winner was Shelly for ugly shoes. All hail, generic! Say 'generic' guys!"

"Generic!" Taryn and I both parroted back. *I am horrible.* My mind raced back to Father Doyle talking to us in mass the other day saying if we see something bad happen and do nothing, we are participating in the wrongdoing. Not only was I failing to stand up for a nice girl, I was participating in making fun of her just because she didn't have a lot of money. I was so ashamed of myself but put it out of my head for the time being.

Thankfully, Patty soon became bored with the "generic awards" and I hoped to make it through the rest of this night without doing anything else that I was ashamed of.

Patty had a Beta tape player which meant that she could watch any movie she wanted to at any time. We watched *Grease II* while eating popcorn and drinking more pop. I thought *Grease II* was horrible compared to the original, but I kept that to myself as Taryn and Patty were laughing the whole time.

I was getting a little tired, it was already 10:50 and normally I went to bed at ten on the weekends. We went back into Patty's room and got ready for bed. Patty had Go-Go's pajamas—Belinda Carlisle coolly gazing out from her top. Taryn's PJ's were very girly—super soft purple with ruffles at the wrists and ankles. I knew my rainbow PJ's were not cool and Patty could sense it.

"Nice rainbows, Jenny," she laughed.

"Yeah—I was hoping for new ones for Christmas, but, oh well!" I tried to laugh it off.

"I love rainbows!" said Taryn earnestly. "Even if they are a little babyish. They are soooo pretty!" I couldn't help but admire how Taryn wasn't afraid to say what she thought in front of Patty sometimes. It was as if she walked a tight rope of giving in to her sometimes but asserting her own opinion other times.

"Okay—so are you guys totally excited to go skating tomorrow, or what?" Patty asked.

"Yeah!" we both responded back.

"Jenny, did you know that, like, all of our boyfriends totally stopped liking us and liked you when you came to school?"

"Huh?"

"They did, right Tar?"

"Yup," Taryn agreed.

"Oh. I don't think so. I'm not as pretty as you guys are!" I said, not really knowing what to say and having a hard time believing what Patty was telling me.

"No! It's true. I think being new is special…and they were all talking about you for a long time. But then Michael said he was going to ask you out—so the other guys stopped liking you."

"Oh," was all I could think to say.

"But, you know, now you're just, like, one of the class."

"Yeah, I know what you mean," I said, just trying to seem agreeable.

"So, let's all plan to get ready around 11, so we have plenty of time to curl our hair. I'll curl your hair, Jenny. You don't have a good haircut for holding curl, but I think I can make it feather back with enough hairspray."

"Oh, that would be great," I said—genuinely

excited to have someone with more hair experience work on my hair.

We all piled into Patty's enormous, king-sized bed and talked a little more.

I learned that Patty had two older sisters that were both in college. Patty said her parents called her an "oops" baby. I guess they weren't planning to have her. So that kind of explained a little why Patty seemed so sophisticated—I bet her older sisters taught her quite a bit about being cool.

Taryn only had a younger brother. Patty said that Taryn's mom was, "like, the prettiest mom in the state and that all the boys had a crush on her." I hadn't met her mom yet—but if she looked anything like Taryn, I believed her.

They also both told me about how they had a best friend Emily who had moved away to Texas. Apparently, Emily used to go out with David and Taryn wasn't allowed to have a boyfriend until this year. So now Taryn went out with David but Emily said it was okay with her because she had a new boyfriend named Karl in Texas.

I told them about my friend Karen from back home and that we still wrote letters to each other, that it felt weird to be living so far away from my relatives, but that my parents tried to make it fun for us and I was really starting to like it now.

Patty actually listened and asked a few good

questions while I was telling my stories. I liked her so much more when she wasn't trying so hard to be cool.

The next morning, we got up and Patty played a song by Madonna called *Everybody*. It sounded catchy in a way that I couldn't describe. It was like Madonna's voice epitomized everything that I was trying to be—cool, confident, and grown-up. At the same time, I knew it would take a long time before I felt that level of confidence.

We stuffed ourselves with Mrs. LaChance's delicious pancakes until Patty declared herself a total "tub-o-lard," and then we went about the business of getting ready for the Starflyer.

We got dressed and Patty complimented me on my *Gloria Vanderbilt* jeans. I couldn't help but feel proud at her approval. Taryn brought her own curling iron and Patty plugged hers in and said she would do my hair first.

It was thrilling to be getting ready together and I was hoping my hair would come out beautiful. Patty brushed my hair and put two front sections into clips and then she curled the remaining hair under.

Then, she shook hairspray all over my head for about thirty seconds. Next, she took one of the clips out and curled that piece away from my face. "If you want a good feather, Jenny, you have to have your

Mom get you a layered haircut."

"Oh, okay," I said.

"I'll try the best I can, but it probably won't stay for long because it's too heavy," she lamented.

"That's okay," I reassured her, still just happy to have her style my hair and hoping it would last for at least the beginning part of the Starflyer.

She put twice the amount of hairspray on each side curl and then hair sprayed my entire head again while I held my breath and kept my eyes tightly closed.

"*AquaNet Extra Hold* is *the* best hairspray." Patty declared.

Once it was done, I had to admit that I felt pretty glamorous. I sat down and watched Patty transform her own hair like a professional.

She started by curling the front section of her bangs down. Then, she took the sides of her bangs and curled them away from her face. She gave a quick hairspray blast to lock in the look.

Then, she moved on to curl the sides of her hair. Each of these sections were curled away from her face and I could see how well, with her layered haircut, they formed into a glorious wave that, when gently brushed, resembled a bird's feather. It was spectacular. She sprayed both sides and then curled the back under.

Taryn's hair was long, and she just curled all of her hair under—including her bangs. While her hairstyle wasn't as sophisticated as Patty's, she was still so devastatingly pretty—her sparkly blue eyes framed by extremely long black eyelashes. I couldn't help but feel a pang of envy.

Mrs. LaChance took Patty's *Polaroid* camera and snapped a few instant photos of us. We all waited with excitement as the images slowly materialized, deepening in hue as the seconds went on. Patty gave one to me and the other to Taryn to take home. I couldn't wait to display this on my dresser mirror—proof that I was friends with popular girls.

At the Starflyer for the second time, I felt much more at ease. I knew the general routine of what would happen, and I didn't feel scared when I saw the boys coming our way.

"Hey, hey, hey!" David ran over and jumped almost on top of us.

"Watch it, David!" laughed Patty.

"Relax, little brother," said Matt.

"Younger by a minute, but *way* cooler," retorted David—smiling widely at Matt. *Gloria* started blaring from the DJ booth and we rushed out together to start skating.

After skating to *Our House, It's Raining Again* and *Electric Avenue*, Taryn signaled to me and Patty to go in. We went up to a booth and sat down.

"I think I'm going to break up with David," declared Taryn, unloading bombshell news with seemingly no worry.

"What!" shouted Patty, glaring at her. Then lowering her voice to a whisper said, "Why?"

"I don't know. I just don't think we have much in common and I think I like someone else."

"Huh? Who?" said Patty incredulously—seeming annoyed that this was all a surprise to her and was being revealed in front of me at the same time.

"I don't know. I might not like this person...but I like him enough that I don't feel like I like David anymore. But—I don't want to hurt David's feelings."

"Who? Who do you like, Tar?" demanded Patty as I just looked back and forth from one to the other.

"I'm not going to say right now—I'm still trying to figure it out. But ever since I started to think about it…. I realized that David annoys me," she admitted with a sheepish glance.

Patty's face was beet red and I was worried she was going to yell at Taryn. "Why didn't you say any of this last night?"

"I didn't feel like it," Taryn responded keeping her cool, "I just wanted to have fun."

"Well, this is really going to screw everything up! Matt will be mad at you if you hurt David," she threatened.

"Hey guys, want to get a *Tombstone*?" Michael said walking up to us. He caught sight of Patty's red face and said, "Whoa—you okay?"

Patty quickly shook it off and said, "Fine, just hot from skating." She stood up and said she had to go to the bathroom and would be back.

Michael just looked at Taryn and me.

"Well…I'm hungry!" I said.

"Me too. Okay—I'll go order us two pizzas—the guys are coming."

Taryn and I were in the booth alone and she said, "I knew she would be mad. But I just don't like him like a boyfriend anymore. Is that bad?"

"I don't think so," I said.

"Do you think I should tell him today?" she asked.

"Like, at the end?" I asked. She nodded. "Well…I guess that will give him time to get over it before school," I said, feeling bad about always-smiley David being sad.

"Yeah, that's what I thought. I think I'm going to just do it after the last couples' skate—I just want to get it over with."

I nodded my head sympathetically and wondered who the mystery person was that Taryn liked now.

Patty came back from the bathroom and David and Matt came over with Michael and the pizzas. We all ate and talked like nothing was wrong.

I skated both couples' skates with Michael and wasn't nervous at all. In fact, I kind of liked it. "You have on the bracelet," he said proudly as he reached for my hand.

"Yup! I love it," I replied, happy that he had noticed.

"It looks really nice on you. I really like you, Jenny," he admitted, bashfully and I felt a combination of happy to be his girlfriend but scared at wondering if I was ready for such a feeling.

When we left the floor the second time, I could see Taryn talking to David over by the lockers. He looked very serious and his head kept going down. I felt so bad for him. It seemed like he was trying hard not to cry.

The last song was *Rio* and Patty, Matt, Michael and I were trying to skate backwards all together in a line. I could see Patty looking over from time to time at

Taryn and David who were now going their separate ways.

Patty left the floor and went to go find Taryn. I shrugged and just stayed with the boys to finish out the song not knowing what else to do.

When it ended, I waved goodbye to the guys and told them I'd see them at the game tomorrow. I went to look for Patty and Taryn and eventually found them in a little corner behind the DJ booth. Patty's face was red again and she was crying.

"Are you guys okay?" I said, still not knowing if I should interfere.

"Yeah," said Taryn. "Let's go look for your Mom."

Patty took a deep breath, looked at me and did a little giggle. "I just hate when things get messed up," she said, "and I hate how sad David is going to be. Are you *sure*, Taryn? Are you *really* sure?" She pleaded again.

"Yeah—I already did it. I know you're mad at me, but I *had* to do it, Patty. Okay?"

Patty just looked at her and gave her a quick shrug of agreement.

They both made their way to the door. I couldn't see the boys and was relieved that we wouldn't have any awkward interactions after the break-up.

My Mom was just coming in the door as we grabbed our stuff from the lockers—Taryn and me with our sleepover bags.

"Hi girls! Ready?" asked my Mom, oblivious to all the drama that had just taken place.

"Yup," I replied.

We rode home in silence. I imagined Patty was digesting the shock and hurt feelings towards Taryn for breaking up the idyllic "best friends going out with brothers" group.

Taryn was quiet because she knew it would take Patty some time to stop being angry with her. I also think Taryn knew that Patty would never stop being friends with her—there just wasn't anyone else pretty enough to be her friend—so they were kind of stuck together.

I was quiet because I knew that this friendship with both of them was delicately new and that I was allowed in on a trial basis to see if I was cool enough. Saying anything would seem too forward—like I was trying too hard.

My mother drove us home, talking about how she was waiting to see signs of Spring, and commenting on the garage door art as she drove by. "Now look at that one! What is that, a teddy bear?" she asked not comprehending why someone would draw a teddy bear on their garage.

"I think so," I replied, wishing she would just turn on the radio. Patty and Taryn remained quiet and I was relieved when we finally arrived home.

SHAMROCK SHAKE

"B_{oys} and Girls, Mr. Siba has something to share with you, if you could please sit back down and give him your full attention," said Mrs. Transki right after we had pulled our lunches out and started to line up to go downstairs. It was raining and dreary—even though it was St. Patrick's Day. Mr. Siba was our school principal—a large man with glasses, black hair and a perpetual smile.

"Hello, ladies and gentlemen. I would like you to put your lunches away and save them to bring back home today."

We all started to look at one another with puzzled expressions. *Didn't we get to eat lunch today? Were we in trouble?*

"Children, have you ever heard of the phrase, 'random acts of kindness'?" he inquired.

We all were a little nervous still and were looking

around at each other. Since the word "kind" was mentioned, however, we collectively guessed we weren't in trouble.

David raised his hand and Mr. Siba said, "Yes, go ahead Mr. Rubinski."

David said, "Well, it's when someone does something nice just kinda outta the blue. Not because they want something, or someone did something nice to them, just because they want to make someone happy."

"Mr. Rubinski, that is *exactly*, right!" proclaimed Mr. Siba. "I hope all of you will remember this day and perform many random acts of kindness of your own doing. But…today, ladies and gentlemen, you are on the *receiving* end of a VERY big act of kindness."

We all kept looking around at each other, now so excited at what the kind act could be.

Mr. Siba continued, "A very generous parishioner, who would like to remain anonymous, has bought the whole school *McDonalds* lunch today—and *Shamrock Shakes!*"

We continued to look at one another: *Is this for real? Or a joke?*

"I'm totally serious, kids! You're all getting *McDonalds!*" said Mr. Siba, reading our minds.

And then, walking in through the door, were two

men carrying boxes that contained hamburgers, fries and *Shamrock Shakes*. We greeted this with hoots and hollers.

I can't believe it! I happily put my crumpled brown lunch bag back under my desk as the smell of the hamburgers and fries permeated the air. Instantly, I was famished and couldn't wait to dig in. There were a few giggles as we passed the burgers, fries and shakes from the front of the rows to the back like an assembly line, still not believing our luck.

When, at last, I was done passing, I received my own hamburger, fries and *Shamrock Shake*, and dug in with vigor. First, a huge bite of the savory burger followed by a big gulp of the thick, cold, minty, *Shamrock Shake. Oh—heaven!*

Mr. Siba told us that after we ate, he would like us to spend our recess time making a thank you card for the wonderful person who made the day of all the first through eighth graders at St. Liborius school and gave us a beautiful example of "random acts of kindness."

That seemed like the least we could do! That person probably spent five hundred dollars on us—how amazing. I felt so lucky and cared for to go to this school where there was a kind person who just wanted to make all the kids happy for a day.

Growing up, I enjoyed all the schools that I had gone to over the years—but St. Liborius was proving to be extra special. For example—we had "take out" hot lunches instead of normal cafeteria food. St. Liborius didn't bother with cooking and would instead order take out on the hot lunch days. Sometimes, we would get pizza from the *Brown Onion* (which never sounded like an appetizing restaurant name to me—but their pizza was great!) Or, my absolute favorite, *Kentucky Fried Chicken*. If I somehow forgot to order hot lunch for *Kentucky Fried Chicken* day, I would almost be in tears as my classmates would open their individual boxes which contained a steaming piece of fried chicken, mashed potatoes, gravy and a biscuit. Cold, limp sandwiches would just seem tortuous to endure on *Kentucky Fried Chicken* days.

We also had unusual assemblies—which included talent shows, movies, and themed bake sales. Sometimes, Mr. Siba would just gather us all together—postponing whatever schoolwork there was—and tell the whole school stories. Those were my absolute favorite.

After being a student at St. Liborius for seven months, I felt pretty much at home and like I was just one of the gang. I blended in now. It was great.

The basketball season was almost over—we were in second place behind Mount Carmel. Cheerleading for the games became more and more fun as the cheers became second nature now and going out to the center of the court to do routines during timeouts and halftime was fun instead of being scary.

Miss Becky told us that next year, we would be entering the cheerleading "competition." She explained that this is where the cheerleading squads in the county would come and compete. The winners would get a trophy to bring back to the school. Next year, she warned, we would have an extra practice during the two months leading up to competition. I fantasized about handing Mr. Siba a huge, first place trophy to put in our school's trophy case.

It had been almost a month since the big break up. David and Taryn had managed to go back to being good friends and it was almost as if they had never gone out in the first place. Patty was still going out with Matt and, because everyone was still friends, she was happy.

I was still going out with Michael but beginning to get an itchy feeling like I didn't want to anymore. There were so many cute boys in our class like Mark and David, that I was feeling a little restless to be Michael's girlfriend for so long. The problem was, we hadn't gone to the Starflyer because there had been games every Saturday and I just didn't know where or how I would break up with Michael.

One day, I asked Liz about it at recess. "Hmm— that's a tough one. I don't know what you should do. Why don't you like him—he seems so nice?" she wondered.

"I know. He *is* so nice. It's not like I want to break up with him because I *don't* like him. I dunno…I guess I just feel funny being his girlfriend for so long. I'm only in fifth grade and I think other guys are cute too. I just want to be *me* again—Jenny—not Michael Bucknell's girlfriend, ya know?"

"I guess. So…who do you think is cute?" she wanted to know.

"You know—I have always thought that Mark was cute."

"But, you're like twenty inches taller than him now, Jenny!"

"I know," I lamented. "That would make couples' skate really weird. But his face is *so* cute! He looks like a golden teddy bear."

Liz laughed, "Ha. I guess he does look kind of cuddly…so, who else?"

"Well, I also think David is pretty cute—in a totally different way."

"Like what?"

"Well, I think his face is cute. He's got a great smile. I usually don't really *like* blond hair on boys— but he is just so *fun* and has such spirit, ya know?"

"Yeah. I know what you mean. Even though Matt

is probably more *officially* good-looking, David is funnier and that makes him cuter," she reasoned out loud.

"Yeah! *Exactly!*" I said, happy that Liz was following my line of thinking.

"Well it sounds like you need to break up then," she said.

"Ugh…I know. I just don't know how."

"Well, how 'bout calling him?" she suggested.

I had never called a boy before and calling one for the first time just to break up with him sounded terrible. "What if I just wrote him a note?" I thought out loud.

"Oh, I dunno, Jenny, that might be kind of mean."

"Well, it's going to stink no matter *how* he learns about it. At least this way, he can be by himself." I suggested, trying to convince myself as much as Liz that wimping out with a note wasn't a crummy thing to do.

"I just don't know…I think it will really hurt his feelings," Liz pressed, and, with a heavy heart, I realized it was the truth.

"Uh…you're right. I guess I'll *have* to call him. I can't really do it on the bus or at recess—that would be terrible."

"Yeah, sorry—I know that will really be hard," she said.

Liz was a good friend. I was glad that I could tell her anything and not only would she keep it a secret, but she gave me good advice in a sympathetic way. It occurred to me that I would never be able to talk to Patty or Taryn like this.

Since the sleepover at Patty's house, we had remained friendly—I'd get head nods from Patty and smiles from Taryn—but I still did not hang out with them at school. Patty and Taryn still ate lunch together and talked during recess by the boys. They never asked me to come sit with them which was somewhat of a relief because I don't think I could leave Liz, Hope and Kristen at lunch. That would be too mean.

As I got home that afternoon, my heart was thumping in anticipation of the dreaded phone call I had to make. I got out the phone book and looked up Michael's number and went up into my parents' room to use their phone.

I stared at the number wondering if I should just forget it. Michael was so nice, and it wouldn't hurt to go out with him for a little longer. However, the restless part of me just wanted to be free and I knew I had to get it over with. With my hand shaking, I dialed the number.

"Hello?" A woman answered.

"Oh, hi…um, Mrs. Bucknell?" I asked.

"Yes."

"Oh, this is Michael's friend, Jenny," I nervously blurted. "Is he home?" My heart was now pounding so hard that I was sure she could hear it over the phone.

"Oh, hi sweetie. Yes, I'll get him—just a sec," said his Mom. *Oh, this was horrible! She called me sweetie and I am about to break up with her son!*

"Hi…*Jenny*?" asked Michael, sounding so familiar and nice, probably wondering why I was so bold as to call.

"Yup…it's me," I said, with the pounding accelerating.

"What's up?"

"Oh, I dunno, I just had to call you because I have some bad news." *Oh goodness! Why hadn't I practiced what I was going to say?*

"What?" he said sounding concerned and suddenly very cute. I felt so conflicted.

"Um…I don't really want to go out anymore— not, like, not with *you*—just kind of not going out at all."

"Oh," he said, pausing for a while, "okay."

"But…it's not because I don't like you. It's just, I feel weird going out with anyone, ya know?" *Oh, this was not going well.*

"Um…not really—I really like you but if you don't want to go out anymore, that's okay. Um, I've gotta go get ready for practice…bye."

"Bye," I squeaked out before I heard the dial tone on the line. I felt terrible. *Michael was such a nice boy— what was wrong with me? Why did I want to break up with him?*

I lied on my parents' bed for a while crying for a bit while my heartbeat slowly returned to normal. I stayed there for quite some time thinking while looking out the window at the gray skies. It felt truly horrible to be the reason why Michael was probably sad right now. I wished I could have given him a hug—but I was probably the last person that he would want a hug from. The excitement I felt earlier that day talking to Liz about other cute boys had gone away.

After a while, I realized that if I was being honest with myself, there was a big part of me that just didn't like being "a girlfriend." I thought other boys in my class were cute, and if that was true, then it seemed wrong for me to be going out with Michael. I did the right thing—it's just that it was hard to do. I knew it would be difficult to see him on the bus and at school. But I was glad I got it over with and hoped that we would eventually be friends like Taryn and David had become after breaking up.

"Why the sad face, Niffer?" said my Dad later that night at dinner.

"Oh, I dunno—I just kind of hurt the feelings of a boy who likes me." It felt weird admitting that a boy liked me to my Dad.

"Huh, well…I have a feeling you are going to hurt a lot of boys feelings, Nif," he laughed.

"Dad! That's not very nice," I defended myself, "I'm not *mean* and I feel *horrible*."

"I didn't mean it like that, Nif. It's just, I meant you're pretty and nice and good at sports and funny. Guys are gonna like you. And you're only in fifth grade—WAY too young to have boyfriends, in my opinion."

"Oh Dad. It's not like a REAL boyfriend or anything," I said, suddenly very embarrassed and hoping this subject would end.

"I know. I know. But that's what I mean—you'll get a little older. Well, WAY older, and then you should go out on dates. You should get to know a lot of different people—that's how you figure out who you like. So, you're not being mean—it's just you are too young."

"I agree," said my Mom. "Play the field! But your Dad is right, you shouldn't have a boyfriend in fifth grade."

Now I was really starting to get embarrassed and annoyed. "I don't have a boyfriend. We were just going *out*," I huffed.

"What does 'going out' mean?" They both said in unison.

"Uh, I don't know—just, like, you're *friends* but only friends with one boy at a time."

"Sounds like a boyfriend to me," chirped my Mom.

"Okay, never mind," I huffed, just wanting them to drop it.

"Jenny's got a BOYfriend. Jenny's got a BOYfriend," sang Lala.

"Alright, Lala—that's enough," said my Mom coming to my rescue while my Dad laughed.

Later that night I thought about what my Dad said. He was right—while I was excited to be "going out" with a boy for a while, I didn't feel like I was old enough to just spend time with one boy. It felt too uncomfortable for where I was right now. I did have little crushes on boys—but I was happy to just think about them and maybe just know they like me back.

I hated hurting Michael's feelings. If we weren't "going out" in the first place, I would never have had caused him to feel sad. *From now on, no more "going out" for me.*

March 23, 1982

Dear Karen,

Sorry it has taken me forever to write. I hope you had a good Christmas. We didn't get to go to Philadelphia so it wasn't really the same. Sometimes I start to feel like I am really okay being here now and happy. (Like the other day some person bought the whole school McDonalds for lunch!!! Can you believe that?) Other times, I just want to come back to Connecticut so bad. I don't really have a friend like you here and I know I never will. I have Liz who is really nice and I feel like I can tell her anything, but we run out of fun things to do together. I mean, I can't think of any time you and I were together that we weren't laughing. You know?

Then I have this girl who is kind of scary sometimes, but other times is nice—Patty. She is so grown up and it is really fun doing things with her, but she also can be mean sometimes too. They kind of have been inviting me to things and I had a fun sleepover with her and this other girl, Taryn, but it's just different. They don't really hang out with me in school. So, I don't know. It's all a mess.

And I just broke up with this guy that I was going out with named Michael. He is so nice, but I was starting to feel gross about going out with someone. I think I like this other boy named David. He has blond hair and is tall and skinny but he has a really cute face and I like him a lot. Then again, I don't really want to go out with anyone either. Ugh. I wish you were here to talk to.

What is going on there? Did you do the Christmas play? (I was planning to write you a long letter over vacation, but I got lazy. Sorry!!!) Did Jenny M. get to be Mary again? All the teachers love her so much. I always wished they picked you or me to play Mary. What else is new? Are you doing the paper route still? I need to save up my allowance. I have no money after buying Christmas presents.

Okay, send me a letter when you can. I miss you.

Love,

Jenny

p.s.-have you heard any Madonna songs? I really like her!

RETURN OF RECESS

"**S**o, what happened? Why did you break up with Michael?" Patty demanded to know the next day at recess.

"Did he tell everybody already?" I asked, cringing. I had darted on the bus earlier that morning and sat in one of the front seats so I wouldn't have to make eye contact with him. We had both managed to avoid eye contact for the whole day.

"Yeah! He told Matt but said it was no big deal and he wasn't mad or anything. But Matt said he was really sad. He stayed in to help Mrs. Transki organize the books—I don't think he felt like being at recess," she revealed.

"Oh, I feel so bad," I said.

"I thought you liked him?" Patty squinted her eyes

in a look that was both inquisitive and challenging at the same time.

"I do—he's so nice. I just feel like I don't really want to go out with *anyone* right now," I admitted truthfully.

"Why? You don't like someone else?"

"No. Not really. It's hard to explain—I guess I just want to be myself for a while."

Patty gave me a look like I was crazy.

"I know what you mean," said Taryn. "It's like, sometimes, you don't want a boyfriend. It's nice to be free," she said with a friendly smile.

"Yeah. I just wish I didn't have to hurt Michael's feelings to be free. But I do like him. I dunno—I just want to go back to normal for a while."

"Huh, well…I *guess*," said Patty, still not really understanding why someone would choose not to be someone's girlfriend. "Well, now that basketball is over, we should go to the Starflyer this weekend to celebrate."

"Yeah!" Taryn and I both said at the same time.

"Hey! Jenny!" David hollered over from the softball field. "Will you play shortstop for John while he goes to the bathroom?"

"Sure!" I said as I ran over and John passed me his glove. It was finally warm out again and we had been able to go to outdoor recess for a week now.

Patty just shook her head at me in disapproval, puzzled at why in the world I would want to play and get all hot and sweaty. I didn't care, though—playing softball was way more fun than standing around talking.

"*Crack!*" Mark hit a line drive that was coming about six feet to my right. I kept my eye on the ball and, since I was standing on the balls of my feet like my Dad had always taught me to do, I was able to instantaneously leap right and catch the ball which made a satisfying *thwat* against the leather glove. I then threw the ball to first base and Matt was able to tag out Gregg who had started out for second base thinking I wouldn't be able to catch the ball in the air. *Double play!*

With that, we had our third out and we ran in from the field. I felt a little bad getting Mark out.

"John was up next—so you can hit for him, Jenny," said David giving me a pat on the shoulder in approval of my skills.

I was so happy. I hadn't played softball since recess in October and I forgot how fun it was—it took my mind off everything else.

I stepped up to the plate, set my position and blew out a puff of air. The first pitch was way outside. I reset, keeping my elbow up high and my wrists loose, moving the bat around in little circles.

The next pitch was a little low and slightly outside which was always my sweet spot, so I took a quick swing, not taking my eye off the ball and *crack* it went sailing out to left field. The ball went bombing over Frankie C's head. Frankie was the shortest boy in our class, but he was a good thrower.

I ran as fast as I could to first, then second, as I saw Frankie reaching the ball.

I decided to go for third, hoping I could outrun his throw—even though I knew he would probably launch a good one. I put my head down and ran as fast as I could. I landed on the base—just clinging to the edge trying to stop my momentum—seconds before the ball reached third. *I was safe!*

The guys on our team jumped up and down and were shouting like crazy. At that moment, I was so happy that I was just Jenny. Not Michael Bucknell's girlfriend. *Just me.*

COUPLES' SKATE

"Do you LIKE Taryn?" Liz asked when I told her that I couldn't sleep over this weekend because Taryn had invited me over.

"I do—she's actually really nice," I responded.

"She's not very smart."

"Well…she has a hard time with school, I guess. But I don't think she's dumb," I said, defending Taryn. I could tell that Liz was starting to get her feelings hurt that I was talking more with Patty and Taryn at recess. I really didn't know what do. I really liked Liz and trusted her, but Patty would start talking to me as we would go from lunch to the black top outside and I knew I had to talk to her.

"I just don't get it, Jenny. Why do you want to spend time with them? I mean, Taryn gets *D's* on almost everything. What does she talk about? *Hair?"*

said Liz, getting progressively more upset.

"Liz, I don't want you to get mad at me. I'm really sorry I can't sleep over. She just asked me first. I DO really like Taryn. She's very nice, and I think she is smart in other ways, ya know?"

"No. I guess I don't get it—and Patty is just downright mean!"

"Well, I think some of that is just an act. I don't know, she's been nice to me. I want to give her a chance."

"Well, good luck—see ya," Liz huffed as she got in line just as the bell signaling the end of recess sounded.

I couldn't believe she was so mad at me. I mean, on one hand, I felt bad that she wasn't being included but on the other hand, it wasn't really my fault that they wanted to be friends with me. *Was it?*

Later that day as we were about to head out to the bus, Liz handed me a note.

When I was safely seated, I opened the note. It said:

Jenny,

I am sorry for being mad at recess. You are my friend

and I feel like they are taking you away from me. I am not popular, and I guess they want you to be popular with them. If you don't want to be friends anymore, I will understand. I just thought you thought they were kind of stuck up like I did, and I guess you don't think so. But I am sorry for being mad.

Liz

Liz's words made it hard to ignore what was happening and I was more confused than ever. I knew it probably wasn't easy for her write this note and I felt terrible that she thought I was going to ditch her as a friend. *Did I think Taryn and Patty were stuck up? Was I just trying to be popular and ignoring the fact that they were mean?*

I walked into my house and plopped on the couch.

"Hi, hon…what's wrong?" my Mom asked.

"Uh…I dunno. You know how I am supposed to sleep over Taryn's this Friday?"

"Yeah."

"Well, Liz asked me to sleep over too and I told her I was going to Taryn's and she got mad. She thinks they are stuck up."

"Oh," my Mom paused and then said, "Do *you*

think they are stuck up?"

"I dunno, I mean, I definitely don't think *Taryn* is. She's really nice. But Patty can be *kind*a mean sometimes. But other times, when she is not worried about looking cool, she can be nice too."

"Can you *all* be friends?" asked my Mom.

"Well, not really. Everyone already kind of has figured out who they are friends with at school, you know? They have all been together since first grade."

"Oh, well, couldn't a new friendship develop?" Mom suggested hopefully.

I tried to imagine Liz and Patty being friends. I thought about Patty's fancy house and her meticulous grooming. Then, I thought about Liz and how her white blouse was usually untucked with some sort of a stain by lunchtime, her hair would have come loose from the half-hearted attempt at any kind of style. I loved how Liz would scrunch her face up when she was pretending to be her brother saying something annoying. I also knew that Patty would think it was annoying and uncool.

"I think they are too different, Mom. I don't know what to do. I really like Liz and I don't want to hurt her feelings—but I like them too. I want to get to know them a little better, I guess."

"Well I think that's perfectly fair, honey. You are allowed to get to know different people."

"I know. It's just hard when you know that one friend doesn't really like another. Or that one is kind of rejected by another one, you know what I mean?"

"Hmm. That's a tough one. You know...I think you just have to be yourself and be kind. If Liz has hurt feelings because you want to spend time with some different friends, let her know that you are sorry and that you are still her friend. And maybe you can do something together another time."

"Yeah. I guess that's what I'll have to do. It's hard, moving sometimes, Mom. You have to kinda pick friends really fast and then they get mad at you when you want to get to know other people."

"I know, hon. I'm sorry. I never had to move and I bet that is hard. All I can say is that, if you are kind, *eventually* people will get over it. And it's not like you have to stop being friends with Liz—you still can."

"Yeah, thanks Mom. This was SO much easier when I just had one best friend—Karen." My Mom gave me a little sympathetic smile and a big hug.

Eventually, I went upstairs and got a piece of paper out of my notebook to write Liz back.

Dear Liz,

I will always be your friend. I really like you and spending time with you, and I am sorry if I hurt your feelings. I don't really know what to do because I do like Patty and Taryn too. I hope you understand that by me spending time with them, it doesn't mean that I don't like you. I do. I hope you understand and that we can hang out soon.

-Jenny

I gave the note to Liz first thing at school the next day and she gave me a smile when I came to the table at lunch time.

"I forgive you," she said. "Just don't turn into a jerk-o, okay?"

"Promise," I vowed, relieved that we were friends again.

That night, my Mom dropped me off at Taryn's house. I got there before Patty and when I walked in the door, Taryn gave me a huge hug.

"I'm so glad you're here!" she said. And I felt happy to be there too and excited to be spending the night without worrying about Liz getting mad at me.

"Me too! I love your house!" I said, taking in the very flowery curtains and thick white carpet in the living room that had fresh vacuum cleaner marks on it.

"Thanks! Let's go bring your stuff downstairs—that's where we're gonna sleep."

Taryn's house was a split-level house with a flowery painted design on the garage. (I was a little worried when I saw that as I remembered back to my Mom commenting on the various garage designs in front of Taryn.)

When I walked into her house, I was in a hall with a staircase to my left and the living room was on my right. Half a staircase down was a big family room with wall-to-wall beige carpet, a big TV, couch and some bean bags. I was excited that there was plenty of space to do routines and cartwheels.

After I plopped my stuff down and we went back up to see Taryn's bedroom. Taryn's room was the first door to the right off the upstairs hallway. It was a small room—but beautifully decorated. She had a very tall, double bed with a thick pink comforter and lots of stuffed animals on top. She also had a humongous cream dresser with a mirror on top. It was a very girly room which matched Taryn perfectly.

"Let's just plop on the bed and relax until Patty gets here," suggested Taryn.

"Sounds good to me," I agreed, slightly hopping so I could reach her high mattress. "Oh, this is SO comfy!"

"Thanks! I know! It's *so* hard to get out of it in the morning."

"So, are you looking forward to going to the Starflyer? Or do you think it will be weird with David there?" I asked.

"I don't think so. I feel like we've gotten back to being friends again. How about you? Are you nervous to see Michael?

"Well, yeah. I am. We haven't really talked since it happened. Actually, we haven't even LOOKED at each other since it happened."

"That's right...well, he has the guys there to cheer him up. I'm sure he'll be okay."

"I think Patty will try and set us up with guys again—she doesn't like being the only one with a boyfriend," Taryn laughed and, as if on cue, the doorbell rang.

We both leapt up and hopped downstairs. Mrs. Wentworth had come out of the kitchen to answer the door. "Hi Patty, come right in, hon."

Mrs. Wentworth turned around and I was stunned by how young and pretty she was. She had the same blue, sparkly eyes that Taryn did, with blonde and brown frosted hair that was styled into the most beautiful feathered hairstyle imaginable.

"Mom—this is Jenny," introduced Taryn.

"Hi, Mrs. Wentworth. Thanks for having me

over," I said.

"Oh, you're welcome sweetie—have fun girls," she said as we all ran downstairs.

"You're such a goodie-goodie, Jenny," Patty honked. *"Thanks for having me over Mrs. Wentworth, Geez!"* she taunted.

"Hey—just trying to be nice! Geez!" giving it right back to Patty—feeling momentarily tough.

"Ha, well, you'll win the parent's favorite award, definitely," she said. "Okay—so what are we doing with hair tomorrow and what are we wearing?"

"I have a new shirt my Mom got in Chicago and some new *Gloria Vanderbilt's*," declared Taryn.

"Um—my *Gloria Vanderbilt's* and just this blue shirt I have," I said.

"The *same Gloria Vanderbilt's* you wore last time?" Patty asked, with her eyebrows raised.

"Uhhhhh…yup," I said, feeling like I just admitted to committing to a crime.

"Jenny—you need a few pairs or people will think you're poor," said Patty.

Her words stung instantly. *Patty was being mean. Was Liz right? Was it a mistake to be friends with her?"*

"Well—my Mom isn't about to get me another pair until it is my birthday, so I guess I'll just have to look poor," I retorted, faking confidence.

"Well…we'll just have to make your hair totally cool then," replied Patty, seeming to let me off the hook finally. "I have new pale *Gloria Vanderbilt*'s and a leopard top. Pam brought it back from college for me. It's so cool."

"So, what do you guys want to do tonight?" Taryn asked changing the topic. "We could watch a movie, play truth or dare, just talk…"

"Let's pig out on pizza, watch TV and talk. I just wanna take it easy. I am SO tired from school. That history test was SO hard! It's so funny guys—my Mom was asking Mrs. Bucknell if Michael was studying all night and she was like, 'Oh, I don't know—he never mentions when he has a test. He just studies on his own.' Can you believe that?" Patty laughed and continued, "My Mom was like, well, I need to get on Patty because that girl is not studying unless I make her!" Patty said, laughing again.

"I know—that test was REALLY hard! I tried to study, but it was so boring," admitted Taryn.

"Yeah—I don't know how I did either. I am glad it's over and it's the finally the weekend," I said.

"Me too!" they both said at the same time and we all started to laugh—the tense feelings from a few moments ago starting to ease away.

After a while, Taryn's Dad came home with some pizza and we ate until our stomachs ached. Her Mom got us chocolate ice cream and whipped cream—so we made sundaes even though we were stuffed.

"Wow, I feel like a total tub," groaned Patty.

"Me too," I said.

"Alright, I need to get out of these jeans right away and give my stomach room, let's get changed," Patty said, laughing at herself.

We ran up to Taryn's room and got in our PJ's and settled into the family room to watch *Benson*, *Webster* and then *Dallas*. I usually watched *Dallas* with my parents every Friday night. I loved all the pretty ladies like Sue Ellen, Pam and Jenna.

"I wish I looked like Pam," I gushed.

"No way. Afton is like, *so* beautiful and cool," said Patty.

"Yeah, she is *totally* the prettiest," agreed Taryn.

"That's our goal tomorrow, girls. Afton hair!"

"Yes!" Taryn and I agreed getting into the spirit.

Taryn turned off the TV and, Patty, suddenly changing topics said, "You know who should get the next generic award?"

Oh no, we were back to this again!

"Who?" said Taryn.

"Liz—she should get a generic award for just looking poor—she's a mess."

"I know. Her hair is *so* frizzy and all over the place, why doesn't she brush it?" Taryn said, almost outraged that Liz didn't do a good enough job grooming herself.

My stomach started to get butterflies and the heat began creeping up my face. I thought about the last time when I didn't stick up for Shelly. Liz was my closest friend here. *I can't be a wimp this time.*

"Guys, she can't help it that she doesn't have a lot of money, that doesn't make her a bad person!" I said, with my voice cracking a little bit from nerves and anger.

"Oh geez, Jenny…you're such a goodie two shoes. We're just joking around and talking—why do you have to be so serious. It's not like she's here!" said Patty, annoyed.

"I know she's not here but she's really nice and I don't feel right picking on her, just because she doesn't have the perfect hair, okay?"

"Good grief, relax. I'm just joking around," she retorted, seeming angrier.

"Okay, but she is my friend and I just don't want to pick on her," I said, my voice cracking again. *Why did it have to crack? I sounded so nervous.* I took a big breath and slowed my speech down a bit. "I think you guys would really like her if you got to know her better. She's really funny—maybe she just needs you to help her do her hair?"

"Yeah, I don't think so, but I won't say anything more about her, okay? *Geez*—we're having a SLEEPOVER; you're supposed to talk about people just for fun. You don't have to be *so* serious, Jenny." Patty said with the final word, still seeming annoyed but wanting the confrontation to end.

My heart was racing so fast at the realization that I had just stood up to Patty. While I was relieved to have found the courage save my friend from all this humiliation behind her back, I wished I sounded a little more in control and not like I was a scared know-it-all. Patty had a masterful way of really making you feel like an idiot.

I took another deep breath and said, "Sorry—I didn't mean to seem angry, I just want to be nice, okay?"

"Jenny, Jenny the goodie, goodie! Boy, you're a hard one to have fun with!" Patty responded, half joking and half serious.

"Hey—guys, let's just go to bed and have fun tomorrow with the boys, okay?' said Taryn, trying to make things light again.

"Yeah—all this niceness is making me tired," Patty joked.

"Ha-ha," I said. "I'm tired too, good night."

We all stopped talking and awkwardly settled into our sleeping bags. My heart was still thumping from the exchange. I couldn't tell if things were smoothed over, or if I had ruined all chances of a friendship with Patty and Taryn.

I lied there thinking about Liz and feeling horrible that she was thought of as poor, and worse, made fun of because of it. It didn't seem fair. I was also starting to realize that Patty was hinting that I was not the required level of rich if I didn't have more than one pair of Gloria Vanderbilt jeans. I was torn between feeling like I needed to immediately beg my Mom for another pair and angry at feeling like I needed to get them to win her approval. I never used to worry about what my clothes looked like. Now, I felt like if I didn't wear the right kind or have lots of new ones, I wouldn't stand a chance of fitting in with this group.

The next day, we woke up to the smell of bacon. "Oh my gosh—I'm starving," declared Patty. "Let's eat!"

Mrs. Wentworth had laid out some bacon and donuts from Marvell Bakery. I had four pieces of bacon, a Boston crème and a chocolate sprinkles donut.

Patty laughed as I reached for a third donut. "That a girl! A true pig-out friend!" She smiled and acted as if nothing was ever wrong and that we were all best friends again. I was relieved beyond belief—I half expected her to tell me I couldn't go skating anymore.

After breakfast, we ran upstairs to begin the getting ready process. Everything in Taryn's bathroom was light blue and very girly. It made me wonder if Mr. Wentworth used this bathroom too, and if he did, did he mind that it was so girly?

The best part about the bathroom was that there was a little getting ready area with a golden chair and desk-like area by the counter that you could put your legs under.

Patty laid out the set of hot rollers and curling iron she brought from home.

"I'll do your hair first, Jenny," she said.

"Thanks!" I replied—genuinely excited to receive Patty's expert styling skills again.

First, Patty said I needed some volume. So, she put twelve big hot rollers in my hair and sealed it with a spray of *AquaNet Extra Hold* hair spray. After a few minutes, she took those curlers out and had me flip my hair upside down. She fluffed my hair using her whole hands like she was kneading a ball of dough. After that, I flipped my head back over and my hair was a big puff ball.

"Don't worry," she assured me, "this is just for body. After I shape it with the curling iron—you'll look just like Afton. Although—you really should have your Mom take you to get a layered hair cut—it will hold the curl SO much better." She said this not as an insult but more out of true concern that I would never be able to achieve hair perfection without it.

"I know, I think I may do that before school starts next year," I declared, wondering if my Mom would actually let me cut my hair in such a dramatic way after a lifetime of long, straight, respectable hair.

Patty started taking sections and expertly curled the front hair away from my head, while curling the back under. When she was done, she gave the finished product a good dousing of hair spray and I moved my head from side to side, surveying the result. I couldn't believe it—my hair looked more beautiful than it had ever looked. I was so excited for the guys to see me.

Taryn and Patty then did their hair and we all were ready to go. Taryn's Mom ushered us into the car, and we put our sleepover gear in the trunk. It would be a challenge to fit it all into the small lockers at the Starflyer, but we would figure something out.

"Okay, girls—who are you going to skate with at

couples' skate?" Patty asked.

"I have no idea! I might just watch," I said.

"No way! Skate with Peter, or David—just as friends, at least...they are such funny kids," said Patty.

"And I think I might have an idea who YOU are going to skate with, Taryn," Patty said with a sly glance.

Taryn just got a little red and looked out the window.

I looked out my window too, not knowing who Patty was talking about and feeling awkward that they had shared a secret that I didn't know about.

We pulled in to the now-familiar parking lot of the Starflyer and bounded out of the car with our hands full of our sleepover gear. Taryn watched our stuff as Patty and I bought tickets for the three of us.

Culture Club's, *Do You Really Want to Hurt Me?* started the party off and we quickly laced up our roller skates and got out there.

I saw David and Matt arrive and then Michael, Peter, Mark and even John—which was weird because he didn't seem like the type to enjoy roller skating.

We waved as they all started to get onto the rink

and happily whisked around to *Stray Cat Strut, Safety Dance* and *Rock the Kasbah*.

As Tom Petty's, *You Got Lucky, Babe* started to play, we collectively gave each other the "this song stinks" look and got out of the rink to take a break.

The boys followed our lead and we all plopped down around the plastic booths.

"John Arnold, you are roller skating?" I asked.

"Trust me—I'm *not* happy about it," he groaned.

"We had a basketball party and John slept over. We told him he had to come in order to get a ride back home," winked David.

"That's what I get for my parent's only having one car and having to drive my sister to ice skating today. I think you all are crazy. This is horrible!" grumbled John—truly miserable at the prospect of three hours of roller skating ahead of him.

We all laughed at John's displeasure. He was either playing baseball or basketball—roller skating did not fit into his idea of fun.

I noticed that Michael and Taryn had moved away from the group and were busy talking about something else. *What could they be talking about?* Taryn was so quiet, and Michael was so serious.

"Couples' skate, all you lovebirds!" shouted Peter

like a movie announcer. "Okay—who wants me first? Don't fight over me, please, I am a gentle person."

I couldn't help but laugh at Peter. He was the third shortest boy in our class, behind Frankie C. and Mark, a little round, and had a wild mane of blond curly hair. He also had very big lips which always made him look like he was smiling, even when he wasn't. I don't think anyone would call him "handsome," but he made you want to be his friend because he was so funny and laughed about his shortcomings. I hadn't really known him at all yet because he didn't play sports and he sat on the other side of our classroom. It was fun getting to know this new personality that I had missed out on all year.

"I will!" I said, and Peter and I went off to skate to *Tonight, I Celebrate My Love for You*—a wildly sappy song that Peter insisted on singing at the top of his lungs. I laughed the whole time and didn't mind holding Peter's hand as he didn't make me feel like he had any intention other than to be friends.

At one point, we even sped up and Peter asked Patty and Matt to make a bridge and we skated under their outstretched arms. It took us a whole lap to catch our breath from laughing.

At the end of the song, I thanked Peter for the skate, he bowed and said, "It was a pleasure, madam."

I giggled some more and went to use the ladies' room. As I went by the booths, I saw that Michael and Taryn were still talking. Now I was really curious!

What could they be talking so long about?

Later, after the limbo, several more songs, and the backwards skating contest, the DJ announced, "It's couples' skate! Let's slow it down, everyone and find your someone, someone who is your…faithfully."

David rolled his eyes at the overly romantic tone of the DJ and asked if I wanted to skate to as Journey's new hit, which almost sounded like it was created solely for the purpose of a being couples' skate song, boomed over the rink, its electric guitars belting out with a longing. I agreed, thinking it's funny how I am skating with the two boys that Patty suggested earlier. I saw that John Arnold had taken off his skates and was painfully biding his time in a booth until the afternoon came to an end.

"I feel so bad for John," I said to David as he took my hand.

"Oh—don't feel bad for him, he's always grumpy. This is good for him—you can't live your life by sports alone."

"Well, I think John would like to try!" I laughed.

David laughed too. "Yeah—you might be right. If we were to merge Peter with John, we might just get a normal human."

We both cracked up at that and I noticed that I felt

happy holding David's hand. We were just friends, but I felt secure being with him and liked his sense of humor so much.

And then I saw it—Michael and Taryn stepped onto the rink and started holding hands and skating. And they weren't really talking, they looked pretty serious.

Patty and Matt whooshed by us and then I saw Matt give a little encouraging pat to Michael's shoulder.

Because Patty and Matt were "a couple" they would sometimes skate with their arms around each other's waists. At that moment, I saw Michael reach his arm around Taryn's waist and I felt a pang of jealousy and regret.

What was going on? Were Michael and Taryn going out? Was Michael the guy Taryn was talking about when she broke up with David? Did everyone know this but me?

I felt betrayed by everyone. *Sure, I had broken up with Michael, but was this the punishment? For my friend Taryn to go out with him?*

David saw me looking at them and said, "That's weird," he genuinely seemed as surprised as I was, which made me relax a bit knowing I wasn't the only person who wasn't aware of this new couple.

As the song ended, David turned to me and said, "You're a cool girl, Jenny."

"Thanks," I responded, caught off guard at the nice compliment, "and, you're pretty okay too." *Why couldn't I ever come up with anything normal to say on the spot?*

David smiled and told me he'd see me at school.

I went to the lockers to look for the girls. My Mom was coming to take us home.

I saw Patty and Taryn already taking off their skates by the lockers.

Patty looked at me and smiled, "Peter and David—just as I thought!"

"Yeah—I guess your prediction came true," I admitted lightly as I glanced at Taryn, trying to gauge her expression. She would not look my way and I felt shaky thinking about her and Patty having this secret about Michael.

We made our way out the door and I saw the familiar green station wagon waiting halfway down the parking lot. I waved to my Mom and we all got in.

"Hi girls!" my Mom said cheerfully.

"Hi, Mrs. Foster," they both said in unison.

"Have fun?"

"Yup!" I said, wanting the questions to stop as I

was confused about what was going on and needed time to figure it out.

Taryn was the first one to be dropped off and she said a very quick goodbye. I got into the back of the car so Patty wouldn't be alone.

"Are you mad?" Patty whispered to me.

"No, why would I be mad?" I whispered back trying my very hardest to seem unfazed.

"I thought you might be mad that Taryn is going out with Michael now." *So they WERE going out now!*

"Oh—I didn't know they were going out. I was just surprised—but I'm not mad. It's good if they like each other," I lied—using all of the control I could muster to hold my emotions together. It seemed like she was trying to make me upset. *Was she getting back at me for sticking up for Liz?*

"Jenny—you can't keep all the guys for yourself!" Patty accused.

"I know! I'm okay. I'm not mad—really, I just didn't have any idea that they liked each other, that's all."

"Well you looked kind of upset when you were skating."

"I'm not—I'm fine…really."

Patty searched my face for cracks, but I was determined to look like nothing was bothering me.

"Okay...well, Mike was really broken up about you and it's cool that he now is over it and is happy again, you know?"

"Yeah, I know, he's a really nice person. He should be happy," I said—really meaning it but knowing I couldn't wait to be alone so I could cry.

Thankfully, she seemed to buy the fact that I was okay and she changed the topic to who was funnier—Peter or David. I tried my best to block out the sadness and concentrate on this question. I could not let her see that I was about to fall apart.

"When I think about Peter, I start to want to laugh because he is just funny, you know? But David says like, smart funny things. It's different types of funny."

"Totally!" she agreed, "that's, like, exactly it."

Remarkably, I held it together until we dropped her off and spent the rest of the ride in silence just wanted to get to my room.

After a long, satisfying amount of crying into my pillow while holding my trusty Popcorn, I stared at my ceiling, exhausted by all the emotion I had let out. Several thoughts swirled and started to take shape:

❀ *Michael was going out with Taryn so quickly after going out with me and it stung. Patty WAS right—I broke up with him and he certainly could go out with anyone he wanted, and it wasn't nice of me to want him to just be sad. But part of what I really liked about Michael was that he was so smart, and he seemed to like that I was smart too—and different. It wasn't that I didn't like HIM—I just didn't feel ready to be so serious with anyone when I was only in fifth grade. It hurt to think that maybe he really didn't care about me being smart and that maybe he just wanted to go out with someone who was really pretty. And Taryn was really pretty—way prettier than me. I was jealous.*

❀ *Why didn't Taryn tell me she liked Michael? Was he the guy she liked when she wanted to break up with David—when I was going out with him? I felt pretty stupid that she and Patty had talked about it before and hurt that they wouldn't just tell me ahead of time—so I didn't have to be surprised by it like that. Did Patty want me to be surprised? Did she like it that I felt stupid? Was this to put me in my place after I confronted her about not picking on Liz? I couldn't tell—but it made me want to be more cautious.*

❀ *David was a nice friend. That was probably the best part of the day. I really liked him and felt like I could trust him and that he wouldn't be mean on purpose—just wasn't his nature.*

"Jenny? Jenny?" I heard Lala call from the other side of my door.

"What Lala?"

"Can I come in to sing songs?"

"Yeah."

Lala snuggled into bed with me and we sang *Somewhere Over the Rainbow*, *Tora Lora Lora*, *Maria*, and *My Favorite Things* together as we took turns tickling each other's backs. I felt so safe and at peace next to my sister—she loved me, and I loved her. I wished fifth grade felt safe like this. I hugged my sister until we fell asleep.

THE CARNIVAL

The weather started to get nice and warm by the end of May and it felt wonderful to put the harshly cold weather of Crete, Illinois behind—at least for the next half of year.

I had taken a bike ride with my Dad over the weekend and we stopped to eat some wild blueberries that were on the side of the road. We heard a woodpecker and my Dad made me laugh as he pretended to be the bird with his eyes getting all round, arms pulled in at the side and his head bobbing towards an imaginary tree. I didn't think I would ever be able to find a boy as great as my Dad.

Walking into school without a coat and smelling the fragrant grass and flowers was just amazing. Our class began to take on the anticipatory excitement of the coming of summertime—when you could just taste the freedom and fun.

We had just had "field day" last week, which was a

bit of a letdown for me after experiencing St. Bernard's field day, the school I went to in Connecticut. At St. Bernard's, we had the entire day off and the whole school was divided into two teams—red or blue. We had contests all day—each with a specific point value, which culminated in the grand finale event—the tug of war. After the victors were crowned, we had hot dogs, hamburgers and popsicles outside. It was the ultimate in kid fun.

Field day here was just a half day and we just played softball and had a few races. They didn't have teams—so it just wasn't as fun if you won a race and weren't racking up points to beat the other side. Still, it was great to be outdoors and not stuck inside learning how to diagram a sentence.

There were, however, other fun end-of-year events that were new. Yesterday, Mrs. Transki took our class for a walk down the boulevard instead of having science class. She pointed out various species of trees as we slowly ambled along listening to the birds welcome us like visitors to their home. There were beautiful flowering dogwoods and crabapple trees. There were also quite a few Japanese maples which David declared as his favorite. I thought they looked a little depressing—I didn't like the burgundy color of the leaves.

The warmth of the sun was heavenly to experience, gently filtering in through the canopy of leaves. And the sweet smells of the warming earth and flowers! It was almost like you forgot that there were smells outside—until Spring came along and reminded you.

Today, we were going to have a picnic lunch outside—only instead of bringing our lunch, we were going to have *Brown Onion* pizza, which I was very excited for.

We bounded down the stairs and outside at the sound of the bell, a little noisier than usual. Our teachers did not seem to care—it was as if everybody had silently made a pact that it was now time to relax the rules a bit and have fun.

I went to eat with Liz, Hope and Kristen—my normal lunch crew. We sat down on our towels (Mrs. Transki had us all bring in a beach towel from home to sit on) and I carefully tucked the sides of my skirt over my knees so that my underwear wouldn't show. The teachers came around and passed out two slices of pizza on a paper plate, a napkin and a can of *Sprite*.

"Mmmmmm-this is soooo good," I mumbled happily with my mouth full. The pizza was barely warm—but it still tasted heavenly with the sweet tomato and gooey cheese hitting my taste buds. I was, as usual, ravenously hungry by lunchtime—my stomach was growling in protest.

"I know, *Brown Onion* pizza is the BEST!" agreed Liz. The four of us were silent for a while as we relaxed and ate in complete peace—just enjoying the pleasure of eating the delicious lunch in the warm sunshine.

"So—I counted my money last night, and I have eleven dollars to spend for each night of the Carnival," declared Liz after she finished her last bite.

"Wow! Are you going every night?" I asked.

"Yup! Me and Mike just walk over—my Mom just lets us go."

"You are so lucky you can walk over—I would love to go every night! I think we are just going on Friday and I only have eight dollars," I said, sad that I had not thought to start saving earlier.

They had begun talking about the Carnival at mass the last few weekends. I learned that it was one of the biggest fundraisers for the school and that they closed all the parking lots and had tons of rides and food. I couldn't wait to go—it would take place the Friday to Sunday after the last day of school.

As we were talking about the Carnival, groups started popping up, plates were thrown into the garbage and towels were tossed to the side. A softball game started, and I grabbed my mitt to join in and waved goodbye to the girls. I had been informed by David about a month ago that I was now considered a decent player and the guys wanted me to play at recess—so I always had my mitt in my backpack from that point forward.

I usually played in centerfield because I was good at catching balls hit into the outfield—but if John Arnold wasn't at school, they would let me play third base—which was the position held by my favorite *Phillies* baseball player—Mike Schmidt.

John was here today, though, so I did my outfield duty and caught four fly balls—one of them being a really hard-hit line-drive hit by Matt.

"Whoa—nice catch!" cheered David—impressed at my ability and thrilled to have his brother out.

As the bell rang, David walked in with me and asked if I was going to the Carnival.

"Yeah—going Friday. You?" I asked.

"Yeah—we're going Friday and Saturday. I can't wait…see you Friday."

"Yup!" I said happily. Over the last month, ever since our couples' skate, I had begun talking to David more and more. He was becoming my favorite person to talk to—even more than any of the girls. It was just so easy to hang out with him and we seemed to find all the same things funny. For example, we both agreed that *Lolly, Lolly, Lolly, Get Your Adverbs Here* was the best *Schoolhouse Rock* song. He now would walk by me at the beginning of each day and say, "Lolly, Lolly, Lolly" and I would reply with "Get your adverbs here" and then we'd laugh.

David, more than any other of the boys, was the proudest of my softball skills. He was always hooting and hollering when I pulled off a good catch or hit a line-drive past the shortstop. I was overjoyed that he thought of me as one of the guys.

I noticed that David used every free second in class to work on his homework. Some days, he reached his goal of getting it all done so he didn't have to bring any books home with him. That really impressed me. I, on the other hand, was a little lazy about my free moments in the classroom—prone to daydreaming about how my hair would look if I had it layered or how I couldn't wait to have *Doritos* when I got home.

It was 83 degrees on the last day of school and the energy level was electric. Mrs. Transki had opened all the windows as far as they would go but there was no breeze to cool the room down.

Mrs. Transki asked Scott Clark for his books so she could demonstrate what she would like us to work on. She shook the loose papers from each book into the huge trash barrel and then placed each one along the length of the table. We were then each assigned to go through our desks and place our cleaned-out books on the corresponding stacks on the back table. Anything we wanted to bring home must go in our backpack, everything else was to go in the trash bin.

We had an hour to complete this job and, as a treat, Mrs. T put on the Go-Go's album and it instantly felt like a party. We took our time talking and pointing out puffy rainbow stickers and barrettes we thought were long lost. A few of the boys found a bouncy ball and were throwing it around to each other. Every once in a while, Mrs. Transki would tell us to get back to the task at hand, but otherwise, she was pretty preoccupied checking off the names inside the books with her list to make sure the entire inventory was accounted for.

After we finished stuffing five full trash bags and two trash bins full of old notes, broken pencils, balled up paper and well-worn erasers, we were invited to the auditorium for a final assembly.

"Ladies and gentlemen let's settle down," said Mr. Siba, our school principal, from the center of the stage. He didn't need a microphone because he was sizable man with a powerful voice.

We all took our places and sat down on the floor crossing our legs. Eventually the giggles and shouts died down and Mr. Siba began his announcements.

"It's been a wonderful year, children. I hope you have enjoyed it as much as I have. Each year is a chance to grow and learn. Think back to your worries at the beginning of the year...weren't they silly? Haven't you come so far?"

I thought back to how scared I was in my yellow dress on the first day. It seemed like it was so long ago and hard to believe it had been less than a year since I had moved halfway across the country. I now felt so comfortable here—it felt like home.

"As you set out this summer, keep God close with you. Remember who you are, practice random acts of kindness and know that I expect only the best from each of you as a St. Liborius student. Treat each other with love and respect. And make sure to have lots of popsicles, swim, make a fort, hug your family and do lots of exploring. Our eighth graders will be leaving us for high school next year and I wish them all the best of luck."

We all looked back at the oldest students—the leaders—of St. Liborius sitting in the back of the room. They now looked too old to be in elementary school. We clapped for them, knowing they had completed eight years at this school. Some of them had tears in their eyes.

"For the rest of you, I look forward to seeing you next year after a long rest this summer. All the best to you and your families...haaaapy...Suuuummer, children!" Mr. Siba roared like a lion and we all cheered back in complete glee.

We were dismissed from the auditorium and left halfway through the day for our summer break.

In a happy daze, I walked to my bus and got on. Michael gave me a small smile—we seemed to have gotten over our awkward break up. He was now fully Taryn's boyfriend and we could go back to being friends.

As my bus pulled up to my house, I saw Lala outside attempting a somersault. She had both arms stiffly at her side, her body bent in half with her head touching the grass and then she pushed her legs so that, instead of rolling like a ball, she fell over painfully like a deck of cards—flat on her back. When she caught sight of the bus, she started jumping up and down hysterically waving, seemingly not fazed by the stiff landing.

Lala's little girl excitement might have embarrassed me before, but I didn't care now. I said goodbye to the bus driver and walked over to my cute sister who was so happy to see me and gave her a big hug.

"Summer, Jenny!" she yelled.

"I know, Lala! Isn't it great?" I said as we marched into the house, hand-in-hand, like two bandits about to set out on adventure.

"Well if it isn't my summer girl," my Mom said with a big smile as I walked in the door.

"Hi Mom."

"Are you so happy?"

"Yes!" I said dreamily—the full reality of a summer off from school starting to slowly sink in.

"Aww—I'm happy for you, you made it! Next

year—you'll be in sixth grade! Wow!" she said taking in how old her children were getting.

"I know—but until then—I don't want to think of ANY grade! Just swimming in the pool and doing nothing!"

"I don't blame you. Well, go have some ice cream and we'll head out to the Carnival around 6:30 after dinner," she said.

I pulled out my favorite blue plastic bowl and scooped a very generous portion of mint chocolate chip ice cream. Then I grabbed a few pretzel sticks and put them on top. I liked to start by taking each pretzel stick and dipping it into the ice cream and using it as a spoon for a while, and then I would eat the two together. *Yum.*

Outside, it was hot and there were no large trees for shade, but I didn't care—I had no school. I wondered what we would do this summer besides going to the pool. I knew we were going to my Aunt Ellie's wedding in Drexel Hill and then to the New Jersey Shore in July—that would be so fun. *But what would the rest of the summer hold? Would I see anyone from school? Did everyone go their separate ways for the summer?*

Lala and I played outside for the rest of the afternoon and then I took a shower to get ready for the Carnival. My Mom had recently gone shopping and bought me a few summer clothes—my shorts from last summer were way too high up on my legs now. I think I had grown two inches this year—I was sadly taller than most of the boy except the twins and John Arnold.

I picked the navy shorts and matching navy and white striped shirt to wear. I decided to do my hair in a French braid since it was so hot outside and I didn't think curls would stay in with this hot weather—even with all the *AquaNet* in the world.

"Niffer, Lala, let's go!" my Dad said.

"Coming!" we both yelled and ran down the stairs. It had been a while since we had gone anywhere together at night with our whole family. Normally, the only places we went to were church or occasionally out for pizza.

"I wanna get cotton candy!" said Lala in the car— her eyes very round with excitement.

"You can have cotton candy, Lala," said my Mom, happy to see her so excited.

"When we get there, is it okay if I walk around with Liz?" I asked—a little worried I would hurt their feelings.

"What?" said my Dad "You're not going to hang out with me?"

Instantly I felt guilty. "I'm sorry, Dad. I'll stay with you," I said—wishing I hadn't brought it up as I hated to hurt his feelings.

"I'm just kidding, Nif. You can hang out with *Liz*." He made a silly face when he said her name. "But when you want to hang out with REALLY cool people—come back and find us."

I laughed, "Okay, Dad."

When we pulled in the boulevard, Lala and I started to clap excitedly and bounce up and down. There were tons of cars lining the streets and bunches of people walking in the direction of the school. We found a spot at the beginning of the street and started out to join the crowds. My Dad gave me a ten-dollar bill and congratulated me on getting such good grades on my report card.

"Oh, thanks, Dad! Thanks Mom!" I cheered. Ten dollars would mean I could go on rides all night long! I couldn't believe it.

"Just meet us back here at this tree at 8:30, if we don't see you, okay?"

"Yup," I said looking around trying to find familiar faces. I couldn't believe that our school parking lot had been transformed into a wonderland of rides and flashing lights.

"Cotton candy!" Lala screamed—pointing to a booth with huge clouds of fluffy pink and blue sugar sitting aloft white paper cones.

"Okay—Lala, let's go get your cotton candy," my Dad said holding little Kirk in his arms who was amazed—his head whipping around to look from one twinkly light to the next.

I saw Liz over by the *Tilt A Whirl* and said a quick, "Bye guys—I see Liz."

"Bye Nif. 8:30—by the tree."

"Yup," I yelled back, already halfway over to Liz.

She saw me coming and we both hugged each other and jumped up and down, so happy to be at the Carnival and done with school.

"Hi! I just got here," she said, breathless.

"Me too! What do you want to do first?" I asked.

"Well-let's go get tickets and then let's come back here and make our plan."

We were able to get twenty ride tickets for five dollars. Mr. Siba insisted on the Carnival being affordable for all families to attend—so five dollars went a long way. I imagined I would have enough money to get popcorn and ice cream too.

First, we went on the *Tilt O Whirl* and saw that Scott Clark was sitting in a spot across me. At the end of the ride, he winked at me. I quickly looked the other way and pretended I didn't see it. *Why would Scott Clark wink at me?*

Then we ran over to the *Troika* and saw that David and Matt were in line.

"Hi guys!" I said.

"Hey, Jenny, hey Liz," David said with his big smile that took up half of his face.

"Hey ladies," said Matt, trying a little harder to come off as cool.

"Hey—get on with us."

"Okay," we both looked at each other shrugging and agreed.

When the attendant let us in, David yelled, "Go for purple!" and so we darted out for the purple cars all the way in the back.

The four of us got in and the ride started up slowly, swirling us around in zig zagging circles. As it sped up, we all started to smoosh in towards Liz, laughing as we crushed awkwardly together.

As the ride eventually started to slow and we could space back out again, our laughter finally subsided. I had to hold my cheeks and rub them a bit because they hurt from laughing so much.

"What are you doing?" said David, amused at my unselfconscious gesture.

"I dunno…rubbin' them out—they hurt."

He laughed, "You're nuts, Jenny."

To which I gave him a gentle nudge with my arm in protest. I was so happy to be around David.

As we made our way off the ride, I saw Patty and Taryn walking towards us. Patty was in a black top and black and purple striped pants—looking like she was at least sixteen—her hair already blonder from the warmer days. Taryn was in a light pink top and white shorts. She looked absolutely beautiful and I once again felt a pang of jealousy. I didn't think I could ever look as pretty as Taryn did.

We got off the ride and Patty said, "Hey girls! Hey boys!" in her controlled, cool-girl way. She slipped her arm through the crook of Matt's elbow making sure everyone knew who he belonged to.

"Hi guys," I said, wondering if Patty was angry that we went on a ride with Matt without her. Searching her face, she didn't seem to be bothered.

"Hey," Liz said. A little unsure of whether she should stay with this group she normally didn't hang out with.

"Let's go on the *Ferris Wheel*," said Patty.

"Okay," a few of us said back as we made our way over to the edge of the parking lot where the *Ferris Wheel* was in operation.

Liz stayed with us and I was happy that I didn't have to pick between two sets of friends. We got in line and Patty stayed close to Matt—who seemed excited to be in her presence—he kept looking at her, proud to be with her.

When it was our turn, Patty and Matt got on first, and I looked at Taryn and raised my eyebrows to see if she wanted me to go with David—seeing as though she was going out with Michael now. She quickly shook her head at me and got on with David, which was somewhat of a relief, because I didn't want to leave Liz riding with Taryn—I know that would have made her nervous.

As the wheel started taking us around in a vertical circle, rising up to see all of the Carnival, and then back down to pedestrian level, I heard Taryn and David laughing in the cart above us and I felt the worse pang of jealousy I had ever experienced.

I was really starting to feel like David was my best guy friend. I didn't want him falling back for Taryn. I felt hopeless that I was just "kinda pretty" but not as stunningly beautiful as Taryn was. I couldn't make my eyelashes as long as Taryn's were—nor could I turn my brown eyes into her sparkling blue ones.

"What's the matter?" Liz asked noticing my face.

"I don't know...I am just being *dumb*," I said, defeated.

"About what?" she pushed.

"I just like David so much as a friend…I guess I am just worried he likes Taryn again," I whispered.

"Well if you just like him as a *friend*, why would you care?" she said with a little smile.

I nudged her and gave the "keep your voice down" gesture and continued, "I don't want to go *out* with David—it's just that I don't want him to WANT to go back out with her…I'm selfish, I guess."

She looked at me for a while, and with a seriousness that she usually didn't have, said in a quiet voice, "I think you must like him a *little* more than as a friend then, Jenny."

I thought about that. *Did I like him more than as a friend?* I really didn't like the "going out" thing. I just didn't feel ready for it. When I saw Patty and Matt with their arms around each other, it made me feel uneasy. I didn't want to put my arms around David—I knew that.

But I also couldn't deny that it made me want to cry to think about him liking Taryn more than me. *So, what was that?* I guess what I wanted was somewhere in between a boyfriend and a friend. *A friend—but all to myself?*

We got off the ride, a few more guys from our class showed up and they all ran off as a pack to go throw darts at the balloons to try to win prizes.

Patty and Taryn said they wanted to get funnel cakes. "Do you want to come with?" said Patty to Liz and me. I was happy she included Liz.

I looked at Liz and could tell she had about had her fill of trying to act cool, so I said, "No—I think we're going to go sit down for a bit," and told them we'd see them around. Patty smiled at us both and waved goodbye. *She really could surprise you and be very nice sometimes.*

Liz and I wandered over to the fire escape and sat down on the landing with our legs dangling over the edge and our arms hanging over the railing. The heat of the day was just starting to lessen into that perfectly warm, sweet air—thick with promise.

"Do you think you're going to wind up spending a lot of time with them this summer?" asked Liz, suddenly just as vulnerable as I had been when I was talking about David.

I looked at her and felt her sadness. I could tell that she was worried about our friendship changing. I had no idea what the future held. I didn't know if I would see Patty and Taryn this summer. I didn't even know if I wanted to. *Did I?*

Taryn and Patty were exciting, cool, and hung out with the boys. I loved doing hair together and dressing up to go skating—it was so grown up and that feeling was irresistible. I wasn't quite sure where I stood with them but, if I was being honest with myself, I knew I wanted more of that excitement. *Could I continue to be more comfortable standing up to Patty when she wasn't being nice? Could I change her a little for the better?*

I also liked the safety of Liz's friendship—I never felt like Liz would purposely try to hurt my feelings. I could totally just be myself around her and say anything without worrying about what she would think. Sometimes, though, I felt like we didn't have a lot in common, and we would run out of fun things to do when we were hanging out. *Would she ever change her feelings about Patty and Taryn?*

Maybe next year would be different. If I could just get them to see the good parts about each other, maybe it was possible for us all to be friends. We did ride the *Ferris Wheel* together, after all.

"I don't know…all I know is that I like being your friend—I'm pretty sure that won't change," I declared, hoping it would be the truth.

She nodded with a slight smile, seeming satisfied with that answer for the time being.

It made me wonder, though. *What would sixth grade be like? Would I pick up with David where we were now, or would we drift apart this summer? Would it be the best year ever? It might!* Until then, I would have to wait and see.

We sat there for a while, lingering in comfortable silence, taking in the festive scene before us: Little kids on the shoulders of their parents, people screaming in delight from the thrill of gravity, and classmates running around with smiles on their faces—happy to be together to celebrate the night of freedom, with a bank of long summer days in their pockets.

A NOTE TO READERS:

I hope you have enjoyed reading about Jenny's fifth grade year in a new school. This book is set in the early 1980's. My dream, (is it CRAZY?) is for mothers and daughters to do a book club together—comparing how things are now—versus then. *Did your mom have a perm? Did she like Rick Springfield?* Ask her!

Alternatively, especially in the era of girl dad's, it could be a father/daughter read too! Or grandparent or caregiver. I encourage a good discussion among generations.

While technology, music, celebrities, buzz words and styles have undoubtedly changed through the years, there will always be friendship triangles, first crushes, awkward moments and popularity! Let the fun talks begin 😊

BOOK CLUB QUESTIONS:

Here are some starter questions for you. Adults—try and answer these questions from the perspective of when you were in fifth grade. Don't forget to add in your own!

Chapter 1

1) How was Jenny feeling about moving?

2) What did she like about her new house? What was a disappointment?

3) Have you ever had to move before?

4) If yes, what feelings did you have? Were you nervous, scared, excited? A little of each? What was hard to leave behind?

5) If you have always lived in the same place, how would you react if your parents told you that you would be moving to a new state?

Chapter 2

1) Do you think Jenny is happy in Crete?

2) How would Jenny communicate with Karen using today's technology? Do you think that would make being far apart easier or harder?

3) Are there things you would change about where you live? What are they?

Chapter 3

1) What were Jenny's hobbies before cheerleading?

2) What are your hobbies?

3) Are your hobbies a big part of your identity?

4) Do you think hobbies are different today? Why?

Chapter 4

1) How would you describe Jenny the night before school?

2) How would you deal with not having the same uniform as everyone else?

3) What was good and what was hard about Jenny's first day?

4) Have you ever gone to something where you didn't know anyone? If so, was it scary?

Chapter 5

1) What do you think about Jenny's observation of the cute boys in her class?

2) Why does Jenny feel more grown up now?

3) Do kids in your class have "crushes?"

4) Are there any fun jobs you get to do in your classroom?

Chapter 6

1) Why was Jenny starting to feel uncomfortable around her neighbor?

2) What qualities does Liz have that Jenny likes?

3) Do you think Jenny was rude in refusing to drink the milk?

4) Have you ever had a play date or sleepover with someone where you felt uncomfortable? How did you handle it?

Chapter 7

1) What does it mean to be popular?

2) Are there certain qualities that most popular kids have?

3) Why is Jenny uncomfortable to tell Liz, Hope and Kristen that she was asked to go to the Starflyer?

4) Why is it hard for Jenny to ask her parents to go skating?

5) What is the toughest question you've ever had to ask an adult and why?

Chapter 8

1) What made Jenny nervous about going to the Starflyer?

2) How would you describe Patty?

3) Did Jenny want to "go out" with Michael?

4) Do you think Jenny will start to be friends with Patty and Taryn after their afternoon at the Starflyer?

5) What do your friends like to do for fun on weekends?

Chapter 9

1) How are Patty and Taryn different?

2) How are Jenny's interactions with Patty now?

3) Have you ever had to try out or auditioned for anything? How did you feel?

4) How does Jenny feel at the end of this chapter compared to when she first started school?

Chapter 10

1) Why is Jenny so sad to stay home for Christmas?

2) Do you think Jenny is growing up or does she still like to be a little girl? Explain.

3) Do you feel like there are somethings that you once enjoyed doing that are no longer fun? Why do you think that happens?

4) What are your traditions at the holidays? Did you ever have to change them for any reason?

5) Why do you think that Jenny didn't write Karen?

Chapter 11

1) How did Jenny feel when she got to Patty's house?

2) Why do you think Jenny wants to be friends with her?

3) Why did Jenny go along with the "generic awards?"

4) Have you ever been in a situation where you didn't like what was being said, but you didn't say anything?

5) Jenny liked Madonna's song, which she had just heard for the first time. Who are your favorite performers and what do you like about them?

Chapter 12

1) Why does Jenny want to break up with Michael?

2) How is Liz a good friend to Jenny?

3) How do you think someone should "break up" with someone else? (In person? Talk on phone? Text?)

4) Jenny was "going out" with Michael. What are the various relationship statuses called today?

5) What does Jenny seem to be struggling with based on her letter to Karen?

Chapter 13

1) Jenny didn't reveal the entire reasons why she broke up with Michael to Patty. Why not?

2) Why does Jenny like playing sports at recess with the boys?

3) What do you do at recess?

4) What do you enjoy doing that makes you feel most like "you?"

Chapter 14

1) Do you think Jenny is being mean by going over to Taryn's when Liz is not invited?

2) What are some of the causes of conflict in this chapter between Jenny and Patty?

3) Do you think Jenny should stay friends with Patty and Taryn?

4) Are brands of clothes important today? Is there a pressure to wear certain kind of clothes?

5) Do you think kids judge other kids based on how much money their family has?

6) Have you ever had two friends that didn't get along? What did you do?

Chapter 15

1) What does Jenny like about David?

2) How does Jenny feel when he goes on the ride with Taryn?

3) What do you predict will happen next year with the friendships?

4) What has Jenny learned during fifth grade?

5) Jenny didn't have social media. Do you think it will be hard for her to continue her friendships over the summer? Is this good or bad?

SPECIAL THANKS

❦ To my children, husband and parents for reading early drafts and for their spot-on insights.

❦ To my Dad, Tom Faustman, for inspiring me to write since he was brave enough to do it himself.

❦ To my friend Shannon Rodner for reading through my draft and for her encouragement and sweet notes.

ABOUT THE AUTHOR

JEN SHIMAN lives in Simsbury, CT where she divides her time writing, raising her three children, teaching religious education classes, pretending she is Steffi Graf and dreaming about returning to la dolce vita in Italy with her husband, Joe. *Too Many Jennys-Fifth Grade* is her debut novel and inspired from the years she lived an hour South of Chicago. For more, visit jenshiman.com

Made in the USA
Middletown, DE
29 May 2020

96295608R00142